# Brett Reminded Herself That Michael Had Only Married Her For The Baby.

Same reason she'd married him. The fact that she loved him should play no part in their relationship. Not until he felt the same way. If he ever did.

Brett stiffened as Michael put his arm around her as they watched Hope settle down to sleep in her crib. "You can relax," he assured her. "I'm not going to be sweeping you off your feet again tonight. We've got plenty of time to get used to this marriage stuff. There's no rush, right?"

"Right," she agreed. To him it was marriage stuff. To her it was the secret longing of a heart that had almost forgotten how to hope....

Dear Reader,

Established stars and exciting new names…that's what's in store for you this month from Silhouette Desire. Let's begin with Cait London's MAN OF THE MONTH, *Tallchief's Bride*—it's also the latest in her wonderful series, THE TALLCHIEFS.

The fun continues with *Babies by the Busload,* the next book in Raye Morgan's THE BABY SHOWER series, and *Michael's Baby,* the first installment of Cathie Linz's delightful series, THREE WEDDINGS AND A GIFT.

So many of you have indicated how much you love the work of Peggy Moreland, so I know you'll all be excited about her latest sensuous romp, *A Willful Marriage*. And Anne Eames, who made her debut earlier in the year in Silhouette Desire's Celebration 1000, gives us more pleasure with *You're What?!* And if you enjoy a little melodrama with your romance, take a peek at Metsy Hingle's enthralling new book, *Backfire*.

As always, each and every Silhouette Desire is sensuous, emotional and sure to leave you feeling good at the end of the day!

Happy Reading!

*Lucia Macro*

Senior Editor

Please address questions and book requests to:
Silhouette Reader Service
U.S.: 3010 Walden Ave., P.O. Box 1325, Buffalo, NY 14269
Canadian: P.O. Box 609, Fort Erie, Ont. L2A 5X3

# CATHIE LINZ
## MICHAEL'S BABY

SILHOUETTE *Desire*

Published by Silhouette Books

America's Publisher of Contemporary Romance

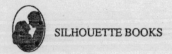 SILHOUETTE BOOKS

ISBN 0-373-76023-X

MICHAEL'S BABY

Copyright © 1996 by Cathie L. Baumgardner

**Printed in U.S.A.**

**Books by Cathie Linz**

Silhouette Desire

*Change of Heart* #408
*A Friend in Need* #443
*As Good as Gold* #484
*Adam's Way* #519
*Smiles* #575
*Handyman* #616
*Smooth Sailing* #665
*Flirting with Trouble* #722
*Male Ordered Bride* #761
*Escapades* #804
*Midnight Ice* #846
*Bridal Blues* #894
*A Wife in Time* #958
*\*Michael's Baby* #1023

\*Three Weddings and a Gift

Silhouette Romance

*One of a Kind Marriage* #1032

Montana Mavericks

*Baby Wanted*

---

## CATHIE LINZ

left her career in a university law library to become a *USA Today* bestselling author of contemporary romance novels. She is the recipient of the highly coveted Storyteller of the Year award given by *Romantic Times*, and was recently nominated for a Love and Laughter Career Achievement Award for the delightful humor in her books.

While Cathie often uses comic mishaps from her own trips as inspiration for her stories, she found the idea for this trilogy in her very own home—from an heirloom that has been in her family for generations. After traveling, Cathie is always glad to get back home to her family, her two cats, her trusty word processor and her hidden cache of Oreo cookies!

For my mom,
who is an artist with a caulking gun and
taught me what she could.
Sorry I still throw a baseball
like a girl, Mom!

# One

The scream woke Michael Janos out of a sound sleep. Even though he had dropped out of the police academy and gone into corporate security work instead, some responses were instinctive.

Reacting instantly, he grabbed for the jeans he'd worn last night, jamming his feet into the denim legs as he hopped toward the door to his apartment. The scream sounded as if it had come from the apartment directly above his. In his bare feet—despite the single-digit November temperatures outside—he raced upstairs, swearing in Hungarian as he stubbed his toe on the top step before reaching the upper apartment and pounding on the door.

"Mr. Stephanopolis, are you in there? It's Michael Janos."

The elderly man slowly opened the door.

"What happened?" Michael demanded. "I heard someone scream."

"It was me," Mr. Stephanopolis replied testily. "I was in the shower and the hot water ran out. I nearly froze my private parts off! You've got to fix that hot-water heater before someone gets hurt."

Michael was *already* hurt—his big toe was throbbing like nobody's business. When he'd been six years old he'd broken that big toe by stubbing it on a stair—he only hoped history wasn't repeating itself.

"Did you hear me?" Mr. Stephanopolis demanded, tightening his bathrobe more tightly around his toothpick body.

"I heard you," Michael assured him wearily. It was barely six and he hadn't gotten to sleep until two a.m. "I'm sure the entire building heard you screaming like that."

"So what are you going to do about the hot-water heater?"

"You know I've placed an ad for a building supervisor to take care of repairs. Meanwhile I'll call for a repairman, but it is Thanksgiving weekend."

"A repairman already came out last weekend."

And charged Michael plenty in overtime. "Look, I've got a couple people coming by today to interview for the super's job. Hopefully one of them will know what they're doing."

Michael's hope was fading by the minute as the handful of applicants came and went—each of them as dim as the light bulb he'd asked them to put into his stove as a test of their supposed handyman abilities. The most recent applicant had all but taken the stove apart in his quest to put in the damn bulb. Now Michael would have to call an appliance repairman in for that, too—in addition to everything else that was already on the fritz.

Meanwhile, the hot-water heater guy still hadn't shown his face, or any other part of his anatomy, since Michael had placed the call at six that morning.

Mr. Stephanopolis had shown his displeasure with the lack of hot water by stomping around in his apartment with his army boots—remnants of the Second World War. He'd had his wife, who was built like a brick outhouse, join him in his protest march. Since Michael was directly below the marching stampede, there was no rest for the weary.

A timid knock on his door was a welcome diversion, until he saw who was outside. Mrs. Wieskopf and Mrs. Martinez stood side by side, clearly believing in the philosophy of power in numbers. The two senior citizens shared the apartment next door to his on the main floor. If their knock was timid, the look on their faces was anything but. "Mr. Janos, do you realize that there is no hot water in this building?" Mrs. Wieskopf demanded.

"I know. I've already called a repairman...."

"We do our washing on Saturdays, Mr. Janos. And we can't get our whites clean with cold water."

"A repairman came last weekend," Mrs. Martinez added.

A fifteen-minute lecture on the responsibilities that accompanied being a building's owner followed.

When he could finally get a word in edgewise, Michael said, "Look, ladies, I'm doing the best I can here."

With a disapproving sniff, the two women returned to their own place.

Michael was ready to call it quits for the day when he remembered there was one more applicant to go. Glancing at his watch, he frowned. The guy was late. Not a good start.

As if on cue, Michael heard the strangled sound of the security buzzer, indicating that there was someone pushing the button in the building's postage-stamp-size foyer. He couldn't ask who it was because the damn speaker was broken, so he undid the locks on his door and strode outside. From his doorway he could see the postman through the glass beside the front door. The man looked as aggravated as Michael felt.

"Got a package for you here," the postman said as Michael joined him in the foyer, his tone of voice making it clear that he disapproved of Michael getting packages and complicating his route. "And your metal mailbox thing-amajig sticks. You better get it fixed."

"It's an old building," Michael said.

"It's a white elephant," the postman snorted. "Axton was wise to dump it."

He'd dumped it all right, right into Michael's unwilling lap. Michael had carried David Axton as long as he could, but when Axton hadn't paid for the security work Michael had done for his company almost a year before, Michael had finally taken him to court—and ended up with this monstrosity of a Victorian mansion-cum-apartment house while Axton had declared bankruptcy and taken off.

"It'll be worth something someday," Axton had told him before leaving the courthouse. "Just needs a little fixing up. That area in the near north side of Chicago is being rehabbed by yuppies. Hang onto the property, Janos, and you'll find I've paid you back in spades."

Right. And he probably had some swamp property Michael could buy for a song, too.

Michael had only been living in the building a few weeks and already he knew he was in for some big headaches.

The slam of the front door told him that the postman had moved on, leaving Michael standing there with the mysterious package in his hands. Frowning down at it, he hoped it wasn't any more of the sex toys that David Axton had ordered before vacating the property.

No, the address label had his name written out in a spidery handwriting. In fact, it had his given name of Miklos on it. No one ever called him that.

Looking at the return address he couldn't make anything out. But the stamps said *Magyar Posta*. He knew enough of his native language to know the stamps were from Hungary. But he didn't know anyone in Hungary. Granted, his parents had come from there, but they'd emigrated to the States in the early sixties, when he'd been just a child.

The package looked like it had come via China by a slow camel train. Kind of the way he felt after a hellish day like today.

Lifting the package to his ear, he shook it and felt a pain splinter his head, making him wince—and making the door slip from his booted foot and slam, effectively locking him out of his own building.

Swearing in Hungarian for the second time that day, Michael yanked on the doorknob, only to end up pulling it out in his hand.

Brett Munro stared at the slip of paper in her hand before checking the address one more time: 707 Love Street. Yep, this was the place, all right. It looked more like a house than an apartment building, but then she knew that once, decades ago, this area off Fullerton had been an affluent neighborhood. Now it was struggling with urban renewal.

Brett knew all about struggling. And when she opened the outer door, she saw a tall, dark-haired man struggling, too—yanking on the doorknob of the inner door before ending up with the knob in his hand. The man had no outer coat on and had obviously just locked himself out.

"Maybe it would help if you buzzed someone else to let you in," she suggested.

The man whirled to face her and she caught her breath at the dark attraction of his face. He wasn't what you would call traditionally handsome, his face was too lean for that. It was carved in rakish angles with noble shadows beneath high cheekbones.

She was close enough to see the striking color of his eyes—a light hazel with unexpected depth. Brett blinked. She'd never seen eyes quite like that before. It wasn't just the color, but also their darkly brooding expression that made her feel as if she'd just been lifted into the vortex of a tornado.

"Where did you come from?" he demanded.

"Outside," she replied. "Would you like me to fix that for you?"

Michael clutched the doorknob to his chest, which was hard to do, since he was carrying a paper-wrapped box, and glared at her. "I've had enough people trying to fix things around here."

"It's a beautiful old building," she said admiringly, noting the etched glass panel on one side of the inner doorway.

"It's a security risk," he replied, following the direction of her gaze. "The place is falling down around our ears."

"Then why do you live here?"

"I don't have a choice."

She made no reply, knowing what it was like to have few options. But that life was behind her now. "So what are your impressions of the building's owner?"

"The guy was a no-good con artist," Michael growled, wishing David Axton were there so he could punch his lights out.

His passionate reply clearly startled her. He saw the way her blue eyes opened wide, her long lashes dark against her creamy white skin. He wondered who she was visiting in the building.

"So are you going to buzz someone to let us in?" she asked.

"Most of the intercom system is busted. Those that do work are in apartments where the occupants are half-deaf." He was referring to the Stephanopolises, Mrs.

Wieskopf and Mrs. Martinez, quelling the flash of guilt he felt at referring to them in such a way. His parents had taught him to respect his elders. But surely not when they took pleasure in torturing him the way his tenants did.

"If the intercom is broken, then I guess there's just one thing to do," Brett said. "Put that doorknob back on." Seeing his distrustful look, she added, "Look, I know what I'm doing. Actually, I'm here to interview for the building supervisor's job. It looks like I've got my work cut out for me."

The man's expression darkened as he frowned at her. "What kind of story is that?"

"Excuse me?"

"You're a woman."

"That's right. So?"

"The ad said I was looking for someone with experience. A handy*man.*"

"You? But I thought you said the owner was a no-good con artist?"

"That's the guy who dumped the place on me. I'm just the poor idiot who got stuck with this monstrosity."

Her look clearly told him that she thought he was an idiot for questioning her skills. She was kind of pretty, with her short dark hair and those blue eyes with their smudgy thick lashes. Seeing the sprinkling of freckles across her cute nose, he was willing to bet she had Irish blood. She looked wholesome. His mother would approve of her. But then Michael had never dated women his mother would approve of.

She was wearing a down coat and a strange woolen hat—beret, he corrected himself. Whatever it was called, it wasn't real practical for keeping body warmth in. Around her neck was a bright-colored scarf that looked like it had been knitted by a bunch of color-blind elves. She had nice legs encased in tight jeans and on her feet were a pair of heavy-duty hiking boots.

"As the poor idiot who owns this place," she said, "maybe it would be best if you conducted our interview inside. It's not much warmer in here than it is outside. Are you going to give me the doorknob to fix or not?"

"Not," he said.

She sighed. "Why not?"

"Because things are bad enough already. I don't want them getting any worse."

"Then how about I talk you through fixing the knob yourself?" she suggested with the patience of someone addressing a troublesome two-year-old who was refusing to eat his vegetables. "I've got a small screwdriver on my Swiss knife...." She reached into her purse and pulled it out.

"I'll do that," Michael said, taking the knife from her. He wasn't sure he could trust her not to run him through with it. She looked aggravated enough with him to try. "What did you say your name was?"

"I didn't, but it's Brett. Brett Munro."

"You signed your application letter B. Munro," he noted accusingly before handing her his package while he turned to the door.

"To avoid your throwing it into the 'round file,'" she retorted. "Experience has taught me to be cautious when applying for a job of this kind."

Michael wasn't really listening to her. Instead he was rather proud of the way he jiggled the doorknob back into place. He had to squat down to see what he was doing while trying to fit the compact screwdriver into the screw's slot. This handyman stuff wasn't that hard after all, if you had the proper tools....

"You have to turn the screwdriver to the right to tighten it," she informed him dryly. Of course, with that he slid the screwdriver right off the screw, nearly gouging the wood on the door.

Muttering under his breath, he tightened the screw and moved on to the next one. Once that was done, he reached into his wallet and extracted a credit card to slide into the doorjamb. Holding it just right, he hit the bolt and opened the door.

"You did that a little too easily for my comfort," Brett told him.

"That's why I've got a locksmith coming next week. I'd have gotten him here sooner, but the guy had a three-week waiting list."

"I know how to put in a new lock."

"Yeah, but do you know how to fix a hot-water heater?" he retorted, certain she'd answer no.

Instead she said, "Depends what's wrong with it."

"If I knew what was wrong with it, I'd fix it myself," Michael declared.

He didn't appreciate the *yeah-right* look she gave him.

"Have you ever been a building supervisor before?" he demanded, taking his package back from her in exchange for her Swiss knife as he headed for his main-floor apartment. This door he hadn't locked, thank heaven.

"No," she replied, trailing after him and looking around his place with interest.

Michael never ' sted a look like that. It either meant someone was cas... the joint or, if it was a woman, that they were getting nesting instincts—imagining their chintz couch in his living room. He'd be called paranoid, were it not for the fact that his last romantic relationship had started with just such a look of interest at his living room. The relationship had ended several months ago in disaster. She'd accused him of being a loner. She was right.

"Why should I hire you if you have no experience?" Michael countered.

"I didn't say I had no experience. I've taken architecture courses, I know basic construction methods. Other girls played with dolls. I played with tools. I'm good at fixing things.''

"Taken apart any stoves?" he asked, pointing to the mess in his kitchen.

She nodded.

"Can you fix that?" he inquired mockingly.

She walked into the kitchen and frowned at the appliance. "Do you have a toolbox?" she asked. "I didn't bring many tools with me."

What kind of question was that? Every self-respecting man had a toolbox—not that he knew what to do with it. He handed it to her and let her have at it, figuring she couldn't mess up the appliance any more than it already was.

While she attacked his stove, Michael undid the package he'd received—which was harder than it sounded, since the thing was wrapped in clear tape from one end to the other. It took him ten minutes to get the outside paper off. The one time he shook the package in frustration, he felt that sharp pain in his head again—almost as if the pain was connected to his handling of the package. Finally he got it unwrapped. Inside was a cardboard box advertising what he assumed to be Hungarian washing powder. And inside that was a mass of crumpled newspapers.

Reaching down, his fingers finally made contact with something solid. Something warm. He couldn't get a good grip on it with all those newspapers, though.

Tossing them aside, he noticed a sheet of white writing paper with the same spidery handwriting as the address label. Taking the sheet, he read:

Oldest Janos son,
It is time for you to know the secret of our family and *bahtali*—this is magic that is good. But powerful. I am sending to you this box telling you for the legend. I am getting old and have no time or language for

story's beginning, you must speak to parents for such. But know only this charmed box has powerful Rom magic to find love *where you look for it*. Use carefully and you will have much happiness. Use unwell and you will have trouble.

Michael had to squint to make out the spidery signature and in the end was only able to make out part of it— "Magda." He hadn't thought they'd had any relatives left in Hungary, but on second thought he did seem to recall his dad mentioning a Great-Aunt Magda.

He read the strange note once more. "Rom magic"... that meant Gypsy magic, Michael knew that much. His dad had Gypsy blood, but Michael didn't know anything about any family secrets. It was just his luck that his folks had recently left on a Pacific Rim cruise, so he couldn't call and ask them what this was all about.

Looking back into the carton, minus the newspaper, he was now able to see something... a box maybe? Picking it up, he saw that it was indeed an intricately engraved metal box, with all kinds of strange markings—half-moons and stars, among other things.

Wondering if there was anything inside, Michael lifted the lid....

# Two

"All done!" Brett declared from the kitchen threshold.

Michael's eyes traveled from the box to Brett. "Wha ... at?"

"I said I'm done fixing your stove. It's as good as new. I put that new bulb in there while I was at it. Hey, are you okay?"

Michael blinked, his head spinning. He felt so strange. Maybe he was coming down with the flu or something. That would explain the heat flashing through his body. It was just his imagination that made him think it was originating from the box he held in his hands. No, it must be the flu. It would be the perfect way to end such a miserable day.

He blinked again, relieved to find that Brett Munro was back in focus once again. She'd taken off her bulky down coat and was wearing a curve-clinging soft sweater the same blue as her eyes. She was backlit by the kitchen ceiling light, which created a strange kind of halo behind the crown of her head. It was just an optical illusion, but it made him catch his breath. So did she. In that moment, she seemed beautiful.

Brett stared back at Michael, captured by the powerful look in his hazel eyes as surely as if he'd clamped a pair of handcuffs around her wrists. She'd seen moments like this in movies, but had never been the recipient of such visual magic herself. This was a first. A momentous first. Something was going on here that would have dramatic consequences; she felt that in the deepest part of her soul. Her heart was pounding in her ears and breathing was all but forgotten.

Then the mysterious box tilted in his shaking hands and the lid flipped shut. The sharp noise punctured the tensely silent air between them the way a pin punctured a balloon.

Seeing Michael swaying, Brett immediately snapped out of her dreamlike state and rushed forward to prop her shoulder under his arm. He was just the right height for her to do that, she noted, feeling a shiver of awareness slip down her spine at his closeness.

"Here, let me take that before you drop it," she said, taking the box he was holding and setting it on top of his rack stereo system. "You certainly don't have much furniture here," she noted as she lowered him into the only piece in the room—a recliner that had seen better days.

"No chintz couches," he muttered, closing his eyes and leaning back to rest his head against the back of the chair.

*Chintz couches?* The man sounded delirious, Brett decided. And he looked pale. Sexy as all get-out, but pale. Putting her hand on his forehead, she said, "Have you eaten anything today?"

"You sound like my mother."

This came as no surprise to Brett. Men usually thought of her as either one of the boys or the protective motherly type. She'd taken enough guys under her maternal wing to man a softball team. In fact, she was honorary manager of a team called Vito's Market Super-Sluggers. But she wasn't wife material. "Just answer the question. What have you eaten today?"

"Enough trouble to give a man indigestion."

"Have any food with your trouble?" she dryly inquired.

"Naw, I had my trouble on the rocks today."

She tried to hide a smile. So the man had a sense of humor. "You'd probably feel better if you put some food in your stomach," she noted.

"So my mother always tells me."

"What will I find if I open your refrigerator?"

"Your guess is as good as mine. I don't get in there much."

She opted to look in his cupboard instead, where she found a couple of cans of soup. "Which would you prefer," she called out, "cream of mushroom or hearty vegetable?"

"I'd prefer getting the damn hot-water heater fixed," he replied, glaring at the ceiling as Mr. and Mrs. Stephanopolis resumed their militant marching routine upstairs.

Looking at the way the kitchen ceiling light swayed beneath the pounding from the floor above, Brett shot him an understanding look. "Sounds like someone up there is unhappy."

"They're not the only ones," Michael muttered.

"Your soup will be done in a minute. I picked mushroom. And I'll make some toast...." By the time she was done cheerfully telling him what she was going to fix for him, she had it ready, and carried it out to him. "Careful, it's hot."

"Thanks," he muttered.

She smiled as if she knew how hard it was for him to say that.

"If you fix hot-water heaters as fast as you do soup, you've got a job," he heard himself saying.

Taking his toolbox in hand, she said, "I'll go check it out. Is it in the basement?"

He nodded, his mouth full of soup.

"Don't worry. I'll find it," she said with a confident grin.

Don't worry? Michael was worried *plenty*. What on earth had possessed him to offer her a job if she fixed the damn water heater? Desperation, that's what had possessed him. Combined with a lack of food and lack of sleep.

Michael set his empty plate and soup bowl on the floor next to his chair. He didn't remember closing his eyes, but when he opened them again, he found Brett standing before him—a triumphant smile on her face as she waved a wrench in the air. "I did it! Your hot-water heater is working just fine now."

For some reason, Michael's heart sank at her declaration. He'd only felt that way once before, when the Bears had fumbled a critical play that had ended up costing them their play-off bid. Michael couldn't help wondering what hiring Brett Munro was going to end up costing him…and he wasn't thinking of her salary. His ad had clearly stated what he was willing to pay, and it wasn't much, but he had tossed in a rent-free basement studio apartment into the deal.

"You won't regret giving me this job," Brett was excitedly saying, ignoring the fact that he hadn't actually said she had the job yet. She wasn't about to let him wiggle out of their deal.

"What was wrong with the hot-water heater?" Michael demanded, lurching to his feet. "On second thought, don't tell me." He stalked into the kitchen and flipped back the faucet. Hot water poured out. Damn.

He knew he should be counting his blessings as he heard the muffled cheers of Mr. and Mrs. Stephanopolis coming from upstairs. He'd finally found a handyman—only she was a *woman,* one who seemed to have the strangest affect on him.

But it could never be said that Michael Janos wasn't a man of his word. He'd promised her the job of building supervisor and by God he'd keep that promise. But he doubted she'd be able to keep the job. Once she saw how many things were wrong with this eccentric building, she was bound to quit. Any sane person would.

"The studio apartment isn't very big," Michael warned her as he unlocked the door in the basement.

"That's okay, I don't have much stuff."

"It needs work," he added before giving the stubborn door a hefty nudge.

"I'm a whiz with a paintbrush," she replied.

What did it take to make this woman discouraged? Michael found himself wondering. Then he got distracted by the sight of the sunlight hitting her hair, reminding him of that moment upstairs when she'd been standing in the kitchen doorway and the light had shone behind her head—creating an image that had left him shaken and breathless.

She wasn't the type of woman who usually got his attention, if there was such a thing. He'd dated all kinds, but never one who had the passion for life that this one seemed to have. She was a whirlwind of activity, flying around the room—moving even when she was standing still. He could practically *see* her thinking as she sized up the room's dimensions.

"This is great!" she exclaimed. "You've got south exposure on the windows down here. It adds a lot of light, even though the windows are high up."

"They're small," Michael said.

"Size is in the eye of the beholder," she said defensively, hugging her down coat to her chest and tucking her hands under her arms.

"Yeah, well..." Michael heard himself stumbling over his words and decided to pause and regroup. What was it about this woman that affected him so? As she'd just pointed out, she was not amply built, although the soft sweater that matched her blue eyes curved nicely around what nature had given her. She had a sweet face. Sweet big eyes, sweet lips...full and sensual. She was nibbling on her bottom lip as she looked away from him, focusing her attention on the kitchen appliances in the compact kitchen.

"They all work," Michael stated as she opened the fridge and peered inside. "They're just about the only ones in the entire building that do," he added in a muttered aside. "I'm told that awful color of green was popular at one time."

"Avocado," she replied.

"Never eat them."

"I was referring to the color of the appliances. Avocado appliances were very popular in the sixties."

"Which probably makes that refrigerator about as old as I am," he said.

She turned to study him with the same thoroughness she'd given the fridge. The brief animosity she'd felt toward him when she'd been in the vestibule earlier had evaporated. Now she was intrigued by him. That wasn't necessarily a good thing. After all, he was her boss for the time being.

Not that she felt intimidated by him. She was confident of her abilities. She knew she'd do a good job here, in a building just crying out for tender loving care.

TLC was something Brett specialized in. She fixed things for a living—stoves, hot-water heaters, men who needed understanding, stray animals who needed food. She worked with them all until they were well enough to function on their own. Michael Janos didn't look like the kind of man who needed any fixing, however. He was the epitome of a loner. A lone wolf. But even wolves mated for life, she reminded herself. The lone ones were the ones who had lost their mates. Had that happened to him?

Tilting her head, she gazed directly into his eyes, searching for a few answers. Instead she found a matching curiosity. He had incredible eyes, striking flames in her soul with their mysterious combination of light and shadow. She felt as if she could look into them forever, as if at some point in her past she *had* spent a lifetime looking into them—which was ridiculous since she'd never met him before today. She'd never have forgotten a face like his. There was a noble elegance mixed with a raw power in everything from the curve of his high cheekbones to the thrust of his jaw. There was nothing traditional about him, except for the chauvinistic fact that he didn't think a woman could do a handyman's job. Reminding herself of that, she tore her gaze away. It was like ripping an adhesive bandage off a wound.

Tempted though she was to return her attention to him, she forced herself to concentrate on other things, imagining where she'd place what little furniture she had. The apartment—with its single narrow main room, tiny kitchen area and bath—might be considered a decorator's nightmare. Brett considered it to be home.

Michael recognized that expression—the nesting look. Whenever he saw it in a woman's eyes he got nervous.

"You should meet the tenants," he stated abruptly. Okay, so the basement flat hadn't discouraged her from taking the job. But surely the strange assortment of people living in the building would make her think twice . . . if she had a lick of sense. So would the long list of repairs each of those tenants had.

As Michael led her upstairs to the door of the apartment next to his, he felt as if he were leading a lamb to slaughter. The two elderly ladies that lived there might look like solicitous souls, but they were as tough as nails.

He pounded on their door. Nothing short of pounding could be heard by either of them. Mrs. Weiskopf came to answer the summons. "You here to fix my leaky kitchen faucet?" she demanded of Michael.

"No, but she is," he heard himself answering.

Mrs. Weiskopf switched her eagle gaze from him to Brett. "Where are your tools?" she demanded suspiciously. "Is this some kind of joke?"

"No joke. Mrs. Weiskopf, meet Brett Munro—our new building supervisor."

"About time you got a woman to do a man's job," Mrs. Weiskopf retorted with the sting of her infamous sauerkraut.

"Who's at the door?" her flat-mate, Mrs. Martinez, demanded. "You're letting all the heat out."

"There's enough heat in that spicy food you're cooking in the kitchen to warm the entire building," Mrs. Weiskopf retorted.

"Is this your girlfriend?" Mrs. Martinez asked Michael with the interest of a born matchmaker.

"No, she's the new building supervisor. I just hired her."

"Hired her?" Mrs. Martinez repeated with raised eyebrows. Taller than Mrs. Weiskopf by a good half foot, she was also twenty pounds heavier. Her dark hair was streaked with white, but wasn't yet the silvery gray of her flat-mate's. Brett couldn't tell which of the women was the oldest. She could tell which one wanted her hooked up with Michael. The other one, Mrs. Weiskopf, just wanted her leaky faucet fixed. That was a job Brett *could* do.

"If you'd like me to look at the faucet now, I should be able to get an idea what's wrong with it. Then I'll know what tools to bring later today to fix it."

"Later today?" Mrs. Weiskopf and Michael both repeated in unison.

"Didn't you want me to start as soon as possible?" Brett addressed her comment to Michael.

"Yes, well..."

"This afternoon is fine," Mrs. Weiskopf interjected. "Come right this way. The toilet doesn't work right, either. Keeps running water even when no one uses it."

Twenty minutes later, Brett left the elderly women's apartment with their praises ringing in her ears, and their cooking in her hands—homemade sauerkraut in a plastic bowl and fresh salsa in a glass mason jar "because it's so hot it would melt plastic," Mrs. Martinez had said.

Michael couldn't believe the women's hospitality. In the short time he'd known them, they'd always treated him as if he were personally responsible for everything that had ever gone wrong in their long and eventful lives. Now, just because Brett had jiggled a few things inside their toilet tank and promised to replace a faulty gasket in their faucet, the two women thought she could do no wrong.

He felt as if the lamb had just turned into a lion.

"So who's next?" she perkily inquired.

He led her directly to the second floor and the apartment of Mr. and Mrs. Stephanopolis. Okay, so the old women living next door to him were tough, but they were marshmallows compared to the couple upstairs.

He should have known better. Before he could even knock on the door, Mr. Stephanopolis had it open and was kissing Brett's cheeks while exclaiming in Greek.

Having heard stories about Mrs. Stephanopolis's legendary jealous streak, Michael thought it in Brett's best interest that he disengage her from the overexuberant Greek's embrace.

"Mrs. Martinez called from downstairs and told us all about this angel who has come to save us," Mr. Stephanopolis replied as Michael tugged Brett out of the other man's embrace only to end up with her in his arms instead.

Brett was seized by a dizzying sense of pleasure and an even stronger sense of enchantment. Michael's chest was warm against her back, and his hands cupped her elbows. His breath stirred the hair at her nape and sent shivers down her spine. She'd never felt this way before, filled with wondrous excitement and breathless desire—all from an accidental embrace.

"I thought you said the girl was not Michael's girlfriend," Mrs. Stephanopolis said as she joined her husband at the door.

"I'm not," Brett hurriedly said, stepping away from Michael and the spell he seemed to cast on her. "I'm the new building supervisor."

"In my time a girl did not do such work," Mrs. Stephanopolis replied with dark disapproval.

"I'm just glad the hot water is working again," Mr. Stephanopolis exclaimed. "I almost froze my privates off this morning."

"This girl does not want to hear about your privates," his wife declared with frosty fire.

As the bickering between husband and wife continued in Greek for a few moments, Michael was taken aback at the amused look that Brett shared with him. Her face had this glow that raised his blood pressure, among other things.

Brett surprised him further by breaking into Greek herself—a feat that provided momentary silence from the couple before both broke into speech once more.

Mrs. Stephanopolis's earlier disapproval melted as she put her arm around Brett and ushered her into the apartment, leaving Michael standing on the threshold as if he were an unwelcome in-law.

Half an hour later, when he and Brett left their apartment, she'd added a bottle of ouzo to her collection of goodies.

"You're lucky to have such great tenants," Brett told him.

"Yeah, right."

"So who else do you want me to meet?"

"There's only one more apartment left. The Lincolns live next door. Since you're getting on so well with everyone, I'll just leave you to it. Clearly you don't need me to hold your hand."

The concept of him holding her hand had a sudden appeal—for its own sake, not because she was afraid to be alone. Being alone was one of many things Brett was very good at. Meeting strangers was another. "Okay. And then after I introduce myself to the Lincolns I'll go get my things, so I can start working on that faucet like I promised Frieda and Consuela," Brett said.

"Who?"

"Frieda Weiskopf and Consuela Martinez."

"Oh." Somehow Michael had never thought of the two women as having first names. To him they were simply the dragon-women next door. "Right."

"So I'll see you later then. Thanks again for being so sweet and introducing me to the other tenants."

"Sweet is my middle name," he mockingly drawled.

No, Brett thought to herself. Sexy was his middle name. Watching him take the steps two at a time, she noticed he appeared to be in a hurry to get away. She also noticed the way his jeans fit like a glove. "Nice buns," she murmured wickedly, hoping that saying the thought aloud would minimize its importance.

She almost fell through the floor when he paused on the landing and looked at her over his shoulder. Surely he was too far away to have heard her soft words. God, she hoped so!

Turning around, she hurriedly knocked on the door to the Lincolns' apartment.

A second later a young black woman, her long wavy hair gathered in a rubber band, yanked the door open and then yanked Brett inside. "I need some help in here!" the woman exclaimed. "I can't get the water faucet in the bathtub to turn off. We're talking Noah and his ark here if we don't get this damn thing turned off!"

Moving quickly, Brett dumped her goodies by the front door and followed the woman into the bathroom.

"My husband knows how to work that damn thing but he's working a double shift at the hospital today—he's a nurse—and with the hot water finally on again, I couldn't wait 'til he got home to take a bath."

As Brett managed to coax the stubborn fixture into the Off position, the woman made a high-five sign. "You saved the day, girl! Thanks! Now who the hell are you again?"

"I'm Brett," she replied with a grin. "The new building supervisor. I've just been hired to fix things around here, like this faucet. Next time it gets stuck, just open the drain to let the water out."

"I didn't think of that. I'm Keisha Lincoln and, even though you don't look nothing like Denzel Washington, you're the answer to my prayers. I been telling the new owner this place needed fixing up big-time."

"Sorry I don't look like Denzel."

"It's okay. Tyrone, that's my husband, will feel better if Denzel stays in Hollywood. Lord, I could use some caffeine after that scare. How 'bout you? Want some café au lait? I've got an aunt down in New Orleans who sends the real stuff to me, so I can make it up right. Ah, I see you've already hit the other neighbors," Keisha noted with a glance at the bottle of ouzo and containers of sauerkraut and salsa Brett had set by the front door.

"Everyone's been so nice," Brett said.

"They haven't been all that welcoming to us, but then Tyrone and I have only lived here for a year and a half. The other tenants have been here decades. Except for the new owner. He only moved in a few weeks ago and now he's stuck with this old dump."

"I think it's a beautiful building."

"That's 'cause you don't live here."

"I do now. I'll be moving into the basement apartment this afternoon."

"You move fast." Keisha nodded approvingly. "I can relate to that. I moved fast when I met my Tyrone. And I know what it's like being a woman workin' on a man's turf. I'm a security guard down at the main branch of the C.P.L."

"C.P.L.?"

"Chicago Public Library. Anyway, it'll be nice having someone else my age in the building. How about that caffeine?"

"Sounds good. But what about your hot water for your bath?"

"The way that water was steaming, it'll take ten minutes before I can get in there. So tell me, what do you think of your new boss? Is he prime or what?"

The phone was ringing as Michael reentered his apartment. He picked it up on the third ring. "Hello?" All he heard was loud static. "Hello?" he repeated, louder this time.

"...it's...your father...calling."

"Where are you? Are you okay?"

"We're fine. I'm at a pay phone. They aren't too good in Bali...." More static filled the line. "Your mother made me call.... wanted to make sure everyone there was fine."

"We're fine. I spoke to Gaylynn yesterday." Michael's younger sister was a teacher in Chicago.

"Good, good."

Sensing that his father was about to say goodbye, Michael said, "Wait, Dad. I need to know something. What's the deal with this family-curse stuff?"

# Three

Michael's only answer was static... punctuated by his father's voice saying, "What?"

"I asked if you knew anything about a family curse," Michael repeated.

"Purse?" his father said, clearly unable to hear him very well. "No, your mother hasn't lost her purse yet, thank heavens. I'm keeping a close eye on her."

"Not purse," Michael practically shouted into the phone line. "Curse! I got a box from Hungary today."

"Hungry as a fox, are you? Then you should eat. You know your mother worries about you."

"Box!" Michael yelled. "I got a box! A Rom box."

But his father was no longer listening to him. "Oh-oh, I have to go. Your mother is eyeing a statue the size of the Sears Tower. I already told her we've bought too many souvenirs. I'll call again in a few days."

Frustrated, Michael hung up the phone, muttering a few choice Rom curses of his own under his breath. His eyes were drawn to the mysterious box, which was still perched on top of his rack stereo system just as Brett had left it when she'd reached out to help him. While Michael might have closer ties to his Rom background than his younger sister or brother, he still wasn't one to give in to superstitions.

It was just a box. Nothing more than that. Retrieving it, Michael studied the intricate engraving on the lid. There were four crescent moons in the left corner, hovering over a scene that included palm trees and a sailing ship. On the right side, a streaking sun was setting over a line of mountains. In the center of the sun was some kind of red stone.

Holding the box up and aiming a nearby high-intensity light at it in order to see better, he saw that the sides were also engraved, with what looked for all the world like . . . a wizard? Intrigued, he slowly reopened the lid. The strange feeling he'd experienced earlier, upon first opening it when Brett had been there, was now gone—confirming his notion that his reaction was due to lack of food and sleep rather than an old family curse.

The box was not empty as he'd supposed. Inside was the most striking engraved silver key he'd ever seen. It was a skeleton-type key, which looked and felt very old. Turning it over in his fingers, Michael felt a strange affinity with the mysterious key.

He'd always loved a good mystery. That's why he made such a good corporate investigator. Because he liked solving mysterious situations with logical explanations. His fascination with the box was easy to explain. His sudden fascination with Brett Munro was not.

The next time Michael saw Brett was late that afternoon and she was wrestling with what looked like a street gang of young punks for possession of a twin mattress.

"I said to give it to me," she was demanding in a no-nonsense tone of voice.

Michael instantly came to her side. "Beat it," he growled menacingly at the kids hanging onto the mattress, their grunge pants hanging loosely on their frames beneath their winter jackets.

"It's okay, Michael," Brett said soothingly.

"No, it's not. Did you hear what I said?" he demanded of the kid closest to him.

"These are my friends," Brett inserted. "They're helping me move. I just wanted them to give me the mattress because it's too heavy for them to carry alone."

"Who's the dude?" the kid with the backward White Sox baseball cap demanded belligerently.

"He's my new boss," Brett replied.

"Hey, man, you better treat her right." The kid had the menacing steely-eyed look of a pro.

"Now, Juan, you know I can take care of myself. *Two* of you carry that mattress, I don't want anyone getting hurt. You go on ahead."

"Where did you find these juvenile delinquents?" Michael demanded of Brett as the kids obeyed her request.

"Have trouble getting along well with children, do you?"

Brett's observation had him bristling defensively. "I have a younger sister and brother. I got along fine with them."

"I meant now that you're an adult."

Okay, so he was legendary within his family for his lack of "kid skills." The truth was that he was wary of children. They made him feel incompetent and awkward. However, Michael didn't appreciate Brett reminding him of that fact. So much for him coming to her rescue.

"Make sure you close the front door when you're done," he growled.

"Actually we've been using the back door because I didn't want to bother the rest of the tenants," Brett told him. "It takes us in the building just a few steps from the studio apartment downstairs."

"I know that. But how did you know? I didn't show you the door because it's been jammed shut."

"The hinges just needed oiling. Works like a charm now."

"Great."

She wondered why Michael didn't look very pleased with her news. Did he expect her to have asked for permission first? As building supervisor, she couldn't be asking permission before fixing the hundred-and-one things that needed repairing in this lovely old building. Since there hadn't been any expense involved, she didn't think his approval beforehand was required. "Surely you don't expect me to check with you before I do any work on the building?"

He shook his head, realizing she'd be checking with him every five minutes in that case. "But I *do* want to be kept apprised of what you're doing. I need to authorize any repairs that will cost over thirty dollars. I don't have an unlimited budget here. My plan is to fix up the building and then sell it."

"Sell it? Whatever for?"

"The money," he replied dryly.

"How could you!"

"What are you so upset about? If it's your job, you don't have to worry. It'll probably take almost a year to get the place fixed up enough to sell it."

"Do your tenants know about your plans?" Brett demanded.

"Why should they care?"

"Because some of them have lived here for a very long time."

"Look, I've only owned the building for a short while. My first priority has to be a financial one. I can't afford to pour limitless amounts of money into this white elephant.

Besides, I don't talk much to the tenants. It's not like they've exactly formed an attachment to me. In fact, sometimes they give me the impression they'd like to hang me by my toes.''

"If I had the money, I'd buy this place from you in a second,'' she declared.

"You just saw it for the first time today.''

"I know what I like,'' she said quietly.

He noticed that her cheeks were flushed, from excitement as much as from the cold air. Although the late afternoon sun had come out, it was a weak shadow of itself. Winter was definitely here to stay. So was Brett. Moving in and apparently here to stay.

She hadn't brought much furniture with her. The battered pickup truck he assumed to be hers held a rocking chair that had seen better days, a table, some lawn furniture and a few boxes.

"How is it that you were able to move in so quickly?'' Michael asked. "Didn't you have to give notice at your old place?''

She shook her head. "I was staying with friends and had my things in storage.''

Her reply made him realize that, although he had gotten her Social Security number, he never had checked her references, or even asked her for any. That wasn't like him. She could have a criminal record for all he knew. Granted, he was usually a good judge of character, but she'd knocked his instincts off kilter. As soon as he got back inside, he planned on turning on his laptop computer and accessing his office computer to do a simple background check on her—not that he anticipated anything about this woman to be simple.

Following them around the back of the building, he watched her clucking over her gaggle of stringy adolescent boys. They clearly adored her. She'd brought pop and junk food for them to munch on as they emptied the back of the pickup.

Mrs. Martinez's industrial-strength salsa was a big hit. He noticed she didn't even attempt to introduce the kids to Mrs. Wieskopf's sauerkraut. Wise move.

"They're not delinquents, you know," she quietly noted from his side, startling him with her nearness. When she was this close, he got the strongest urge to tug her into his arms and kiss her. Michael blinked in surprise and wondered what he was fighting here. For that matter, why the hell was he fighting it, period?

So what if Brett was different from other women he'd been attracted to? Nothing wrong with that. She was a sexy woman, just the right height for him; he remembered that from the way she'd slid her shoulder under his arm. The top of her head was just beneath his chin. When he'd briefly held her in his arms earlier, she'd conformed to his body as if designed for that purpose and no other.

It suddenly occurred to him that this handywoman situation could turn out to be a blessing in disguise, after all.

"Why are you looking at me that way?" Brett asked suspiciously.

"What way is that?" he countered.

"The old I'm-a-man, you're-a-woman look."

"I *am* a man. You *are* a woman." His shrug was surprisingly continental. "Is it so strange I would look at you as such?"

"You bet. I'm not that kind of a woman."

"What kind might that be?"

"The kind who makes men go all gooey-eyed."

Stung, he drew himself up to his full height, his look now a glare.

"Aha," she said approvingly. "That's more the look I'm used to getting from you."

"You know nothing about me," he reminded her. "We only met for the first time this afternoon."

"You don't have to remind me." She still hadn't figured out what had happened a few hours ago when she'd stepped out of his kitchen to tell him she'd fixed his stove. She'd felt so strange...as if she'd been bound to him by invisible chains. The look in his hazel eyes had pierced her soul and she was still trying to repair the damage. Because men simply didn't look at her that way. Unless they wanted something—usually to borrow money. Otherwise she was just one of the boys. Always had been. With one exception...

Feeling the pain ready to creep up on her like the cold fingers of mist that came off the lake, she resolutely changed mental gears. Leaving Michael's side, she focused her attention on getting the last of her belongings into her new home.

All the while, she was only too well aware of his intense gaze homing in on her. He really did have the most incredible eyes. And he looked like such an outsider, standing apart from the action, watching but not involved in it.

"Would you like to come in and have some coffee or something?" she invited, unable to leave him just standing there. "We've got plenty of food."

Michael fully intended to say no. Hanging out with a bunch of adolescents wasn't his idea of a good time. But for some reason, he couldn't seem to voice the refusal. He really wasn't himself today.

Exasperated by his silence, Brett said, "It's really not that tough a question to answer. Look, I don't want you to take this the wrong way, but it might be easier for people to get to know you if you..."

"If I what?" he demanded irritably. "Don't stop there."

"If you lightened up a little, maybe."

His fiery look would have sent a weaker soul scurrying for cover, but not Brett.

"Yeah, well, we can't all be Suzy Sunshine," he retorted.

She flushed. Is that how he thought of her? She knew he wasn't alone in that opinion. If only they all knew how far from the truth that was. There was a cold darkness in her soul that no amount of cheerfulness could melt.

But the bottom line was that she'd never been able to say no to those in need, because she knew how it felt to need someone, or something, so badly and not be able to have it—not ever.

"That was a stupid crack I made," Michael said, lifting his hand to cup her cheek. "I'm sorry."

Her heart stopped. His touch was so gentle.

"Yo, Brett, where do you want this box?" thirteen-year-old Juan asked her.

Brett stepped away from Michael—silently noting that each time she did so, it got harder and harder. Stepping inside the basement apartment, Michael poured himself a mug of coffee from a coffeepot that looked like it had been around during World War II. Sipping his coffee, he observed the suspicious looks the kids gave him. Each glance held a warning. Their protectiveness was impressive.

When Brett was outside, he took the opportunity to get a little more information about his new employee. "Your name is Juan?" he asked the kid in the baseball cap.

"That's right. You wanna make something of it?"

"Why this routine? What makes you think Brett needs protecting?"

Eyeing him, Juan waited before replying. "Because she's the Mother Teresa type," he finally said. "Too good. She's been hurt already."

"By whom?" Michael demanded.

Juan shrugged. "She don't say and I don't ask. All I know is that since she started volunteering at the center, things have been different. She understands."

"What center might that be?"

"St. Gerald's Youth Center. Two blocks from here. Which means we're close enough to check up on you."

"Do I look impressed?" Michael countered.

"You look mean, but Brett told us that you're not really."

"What did she say I was, *really?*"

"Lonely."

The observation stung. Slamming the coffee mug back on the rickety table, he glared at Juan before making his departure. He didn't need this aggravation. Michael enjoyed his own company. He certainly didn't need a snotty-nosed kid telling him what was wrong with his life.

As soon as Michael got back to his apartment, he turned on his computer and did some checking into Brett's background. He learned that she was thirty and had no middle name. No criminal records. The pickup out front was hers and was apparently paid for. She only had one credit card and that had a modest fifteen-hundred-dollar limit. She was still paying off a large medical bill at a Northside hospital for a stay involving a surgical procedure almost two years ago.

Her job history was sporadic. She'd tried her hand at just about everything, from flipping "sliders" at a popular burger joint, to a stint as a waitress in a Rush Street watering hole, to working in a hardware store. She was only twenty credit-hours short of earning her degree in psychology, from Loyola no less. But she'd been a part-time student there longer than some people were president. She wasn't attending classes now, but was registered for the next semester starting in mid-January.

There was no indication of her having any living relatives and she'd never been married. He wondered why not. With a loving heart like hers, she'd make some man a wonderful wife. She was great with kids, too. And smart. Caring. Sassy. No pushover. And she had the biggest blue eyes he'd ever seen.

Yes, he'd done right to hire her. It had been a wise and logical decision. That was his story and he was sticking to it.

"Are you crazy?" Michael shouted at Brett not even a week later.

"I was just..."

"I can see what you were doing. Trying to get your neck broken! That's much too heavy for you to carry."

"I wasn't carrying it. I was using leverage...."

"Don't do it again," he interrupted her to order, moving the huge potted plant in the hallway for her. The thing weighed a ton. "Why are you moving this, anyway?"

"Because I needed to drain the radiator behind it." Seeing his frown of confusion, she elaborated. "The tenants have all complained about the rattling radiators waking them up at night. The entire system needed to be bled, to get the air out of it. That's what's causing all the noise. This radiator is the last one to be done. I have to..."

He was distracted from the rest of her explanation by the way her eyes lit up as she talked. Had he ever met a woman with such an expressive face? He didn't think so. And all this enthusiasm was about draining radiators, no less.

Today she was wearing a baggy sweatshirt. The color matched her blue eyes. A pair of black leggings encased her legs, the material lovingly following every curve.

"So how are you settling in?" he asked even though he already knew the answer. The tenants had been singing her praises and he hadn't had any more tap dancing on his ceiling or middle-of-the-night irate phone calls. Which left him free to concentrate on his work, which should have taken up every second of his time as it had for the past five years of his life. Instead he'd actually caught himself daydreaming about Brett—the way she smiled, the way she'd looked with the sun haloing her short dark hair, the sound of her laughter, the way she lit up a room with her presence.

"Nicely."

"What?" he asked absently, distracted by the cutest little dimple he'd just noticed at the corner of her lush mouth.

"I said I'm settling in nicely." She hoped she didn't sound as breathless as she felt. Michael was staring at her strangely again. His hazel eyes were fascinating enough as it was without adding that seductive look to the mix. Unable to help herself, she lifted her hand to rub her mouth as she asked, "Do I have dirt on my face or what?"

"No."

"You were looking at me so intently...." He'd been staring directly at that corner of her mouth. She leaned forward to check her reflection in the glass beside the front door.

"You look fine," he huskily assured her. "Better than fine."

"Sure I do," she said dryly. The man was either being kind or he was just plain blind. She knew the baggy sweatshirt had seen better days. So had she. She looked like an elf on a chain-gang crew. She hadn't brushed her hair since this morning. Forget lipstick. She hadn't worn any since Wednesday and this was Friday. Yeah, she was a regular Cindy Crawford look-alike.

"Don't you go trying to lift anything else this heavy," he scolded her, reaching out to brush her bangs away from her eyes. "Ask for some help next time, okay?"

She nodded dazedly. The merest brush of his hand and her knees went weak. The rattling radiators had nothing on the clatter of her heartbeat. She stood there after he'd walked away, her mind racing as fast as her pulse, filling her thoughts with images of Michael scooping her up in his arms and taking her to bed.

"Girl, you look like you got hit by lightning," Keisha noted dryly as she walked in the front door to the building.

"Yeah." Brett dreamily sighed. "I feel that way, too."

"Oh-oh."

"Why is it oh-oh?"

"I saw the way you looked at Michael. He may not have owned this building long, but I told you I work as a security officer at the library's main branch. Anyway, Michael is well known in security circles. Likes working alone, always solves his cases. Nothin' slips past him."

"That's good, right?"

Keisha shrugged. "Girl, he doesn't let anyone slow him down. As in females. He changes them often and likes them gorgeous."

"Gorgeous, huh? Well, that lets me out of the running," Brett noted ruefully.

"Don't you be down on yourself. You got plenty going for you. I never seen a girl knows as much about hardware as you do."

"I may know about hardware, but I don't have any of my own," Brett replied, waving her hand toward her small breasts.

"You never heard of those push-up bras they've got? My sister works in a lingerie store. Talk about hardware." Keisha grinned and rolled her eyes. "We're talking heavy-duty stuff here. We'll go over there my next day off."

"I don't know...."

Keisha waved away Brett's uncertainty. "I gotta get over there to pick out my Christmas present from Tyrone anyway."

"You pick out your own present?"

"Only since he bought me a steam iron last year."

Brett winced in appreciative understanding.

"So this year I pick out my own things. Safer that way. How 'bout you? Got your shopping done yet? Christmas is only three weeks away."

"I know. It'll be here before you know it. I'm just about done with my shopping." Despite the fact that Brett had no family, she did have a large list of people she remembered at the holidays. Since money was tight, it was always a challenge coming up with gift ideas under five dollars, but she managed. After all, practice makes perfect, and Brett had had plenty of practice at making a dollar stretch.

"You know what you're gonna ask Santa for?" Keisha inquired.

The mental image of Michael with a bow around his neck flashed into Brett's mind, followed by a picture of their children gathered around the tree. "Santa can't give me what I want," Brett whispered in a slightly melancholy voice, before dismissing the unobtainable image from her thoughts. "Tell me more about that lingerie shop your sister works in...."

While Brett was speaking to Keisha outside, inside his apartment Michael was talking to his dad, or attempting to.

"Fuji has better phones," his father was saying. "I can hear you now."

"So what do you know about a Janos family curse?"

"Curse? Have you been betting on the horses again?" his father demanded.

"No. I only bet on the horses once in my life, Dad. That's not what I'm talking about."

"Then what are you talking about?"

"I got a package from Hungary. From someone who claims they are a relative."

"Must be your Great-Aunt Magda. What did she send you?" his father demanded suspiciously.

"An engraved metal box with a silver key in it. And she sent along a letter." Michael read it to his father. "Do you know what this is all about?"

"There *is* a spell," his father confirmed before static broke into the line.

"Wait, I didn't hear what else you said," Michael shouted. "The line is breaking up again. Did you say that there really is a curse?"

"Not a curse. A spell ... was meant to be *bahtali.*"

"I don't understand. Are you still there?"

The only answer he got was static.

"Can you hear me?" Michael shouted.

"The entire building can hear you," Brett wryly noted from the doorway to his apartment.

"How did you get in? Never mind. I'm on the phone— long distance."

"I'll try to call you when we reach Hawaii," he heard his dad say over the briefly clear line.

"Dad, wait!" Michael said into the phone. "What about the *bahtali?*"

The dial tone was the only reply. Muttering a choice Hungarian curse under his breath, Michael hung up the phone.

"I'm sorry to interrupt," Brett said contritely. "But the door to your apartment was ajar. You said you needed to approve any expense over thirty dollars and I forgot to tell you earlier that I think you're going to have to replace all the bathtub and kitchen faucets in Keisha's apartment."

Instead of responding to her comments, Michael said, "What do you know about keys?"

She blinked at him. "Excuse me?"

"Keys. What do you know about them?"

"That they unlock things. Why? Is someone having a problem with their locks?"

"What about a key like this?" Michael opened the Rom box and held out the silver key to her.

Brett suddenly felt as if she were on a merry-go-round going at 78 rpm. She was so dizzy she couldn't stand straight. Putting out her hand, she reached for something to hold her upright, but found nothing but air—until Michael caught her in his arms.

The power of his embrace was both humbling and exhilarating. The world slipped away as she gazed into his eyes. He looked as dazed as she felt. Then passionate hunger replaced surprise. Seconds later he bent his head, slowly lowering his lips to brush hers.

What began as a soft inquisition was soon transformed into a fervent exploration as Michael claimed her mouth with bewitching kisses, urgently coaxing her lips apart. The beguiling thrust of his tongue made her weak at the knees.

Brett could feel his heart pounding beneath her hand, which she'd rested against his chest. Her fingers clutched his shirt at the wickedly pleasurable things he was doing to her. This was more than a kiss. It was a complete seduction of the senses.

The sound of metal clanging on the wooden floor echoed in her head, sounding as if she were standing inside the ringing Liberty Bell. Startled, she pulled away. "What was that?"

"I have no idea," he said, his voice raspy.

She had the feeling he was referring to what had just happened between them. *He* might not have any idea, but she sure did. Brett was panicked that she was falling for him. No wonder Keisha had said *oh-oh*. It was as plain as the freckles on Brett's nose that there was no hope for a woman like her with a man like him. So what if he'd kissed her? After all, she'd practically thrown herself at the poor man.

She stood frozen as he calmly picked up the silver key that had fallen on the floor and started talking about it— as if the mind-blowing kiss they'd just shared hadn't happened.

Taking her cue from him, she bit her bottom lip and forced herself to concentrate on his words, trying to match his look of unconcern.

"This key came in that box I got—the one that arrived the same day you did."

Great, she thought to herself. Now he made her sound like a package he'd received in the mail.

"It came from a distant relative in Hungary. A Rom relative to be precise."

"Rom?"

"Gypsy. My parents are both Hungarian, but my dad has Rom blood while my mom is *gaje,* meaning she isn't Rom. Anyway, my folks fled the communist regime in Hungary in the early sixties, when I was only a year or two old. My brother and sister were born after we got here."

Gypsy... Rom. Yes, Brett thought to herself. That explained Michael's magically brooding eyes. It didn't explain her magical response to him, however.

"Anyway, the box had this key in it," Michael continued, "and I thought what with you knowing about locks and things, you might know what this key unlocks. It doesn't unlock the box, I already tried that. Got any ideas?"

Ideas? She had plenty of them. Steamy, forbidden fantasies about him, a man who preferred gorgeous women and kissed like a wild-blooded Gypsy king. "Nope. I don't have a clue. Sorry. Well, I, uh...I'd better get back to that radiator, and then I'll go pick up those new faucets. If I hurry, I can still buy them and install one tonight." With each quickly spoken word, she backed another step out of the apartment. "See you." With a cheerful smile and a nonchalant wave of her hand she was gone.

Not until Brett reached the privacy of her own apartment did she allow the embarrassment she felt to show. She was thirty, much too old to be acting like an adolescent with a crush. There was only one thing to do.

Heading for the kitchen she poured herself a glass of milk and ripped open a bag of cheese puffs. It was her own prescription for stress. After eating half the bag, she managed to regain her perspective. "Okay, here's the plan," she told herself, speaking the words aloud for added emphasis. "If Michael can pretend that kiss never happened, so can I. But I'm gonna do it at a distance. That's the plan." Holding up her glass of milk, she toasted it. "Here's to success."

Michael noticed that Brett made herself scarce for the next day or two, but he put it down to the amount of work she was doing on the building. He hadn't forgotten their kiss. It had been seared into his brain. But she'd looked so panic-stricken afterward that he didn't want to scare her off. Besides, technically speaking, he was her boss and he certainly didn't want her thinking that her job was dependent on her kissing him.

She haunted his thoughts and his dreams. Tonight the dream was getting particularly hot and intimate when a noise jarred him awake. It took him a second or two to groggily identify what had woken him up—just when things were getting good! It sounded remarkably like a baby crying.

Impossible. There were no babies in the building. At first he thought he was imagining things. But he couldn't get back to sleep for the confounded crying. Muttering under his breath, he pulled on a pair of sweatpants and a T-shirt, ready to track down the source of the noise and put an end to it.

It didn't take Michael long to track the crying downstairs to Brett's place. She must have the TV on or something. Or maybe she was playing one of those movie videos with a baby in the starring role. Whatever the case was, the noise was keeping him awake and she needed to turn the thing down.

He knocked on her door. She opened it. The noise was not coming from any TV, but from the crying infant in her arms.

# Four

───

"What are *you* doing with a baby? Are you baby-sitting? Is the kid dying?" Michael demanded as the baby continued to scream loudly enough to wake the dead. "Can't you get it to stop screaming like that?" he tacked on rather desperately.

"I'm doing my best," Brett replied, her voice and expression frazzled.

"Well, obviously it's not good enough."

"Fine," she said in exasperation. "If you think you can do better, then *you* get her to stop crying." With those words, she handed the baby over to him.

Michael's protest was immediate. "I'm no good with ba—" Before he could say another syllable, the baby stopped crying. She beamed up at him as he gingerly held her between his two hands as if she were an explosive device that was liable to detonate at any time.

"You were saying?" Brett noted dryly.

"How about that? She quit crying." Michael looked and sounded utterly astonished. "So whose is she?" he asked.

"I don't know."

"You're baby-sitting a kid and you don't know her parents?"

"I'm not exactly baby-sitting her."

"Then what are you doing, exactly?" he asked.

"Um, I . . . I'm taking care of her."

"For how long?"

"I'm not sure."

Cautiously shifting the baby so that she was perched in the crook of his arm, Michael turned his attention to Brett while the baby grabbed a handful of his T-shirt and stuck it in her mouth. "What's going on here?" he demanded.

"I found her," Brett reluctantly admitted. "In the building foyer this morning. You know I was working on the mailbox thingamajig, stabilizing it with some patching cement where it had come loose from the wall. Anyway, I was in and out of the foyer all morning so I know she hadn't been there long. I was gone for a few minutes looking for a tool, and when I came back there she was. Sitting in a car seat, sound asleep."

"Maybe she was left there by mistake?"

"Who would leave a baby by mistake?" Brett retorted. "It's not like leaving a bottle of milk in the grocery cart. Besides, no one in this building had any visitors with a baby—I already asked. And there was a note stuck to her blanket that said: 'Please take care of my baby.'"

"Somebody abandoned this baby? Then we'll have to call the authorities right away."

Brett's response was immediate and intense. *"No!"*

"Why not? Have you called them already?"

"No," she said, more quietly this time. Reaching out, she gently removed his T-shirt from the baby's mouth. "Look, I know what the authorities would do to this baby. I've been there. They'd put her in a foster home. She'll go through the child-welfare system as another statistic. She's just a little baby.''

"Lots of people are looking for little babies."

*So am I!* Brett wanted to shout at him, giving the little girl a look of unconcealed longing.

Seeing it, Michael said, "Oh-oh. I see what's going on. You're feeling that old biological clock ticking, huh?" Seeing Brett's stricken look, Michael immediately knew he'd said the wrong thing. But Brett wasn't the kind of woman to get touchy about a comment like that. She also wasn't the kind to show her pain so clearly. Something was obviously very wrong here.

"What is it?" he murmured. "Come on, talk to me."

Brett held out her finger to the baby, who cooed and wrapped her tiny fingers around it. "I don't have a biological clock," she said so softly he had to bend his head to hear her. "I had to have emergency surgery a few years ago. A hysterectomy."

"I didn't know. I'm sorry."

"Yeah, so am I. I was engaged to be married at the time. My fiancé, Bill, was a brick about it, visiting me in the hospital, even had me stay at his place during my recovery. But I knew that things had changed. He wanted children. That's why he wanted to get married. It's why any man wants to get married. To have children." Even two years later, she could still hear Bill's voice saying *I can't marry you, Brett. I need a woman who can be a real wife. You know what I mean. I want kids. Every man does.*

She'd heard Michael say enough Hungarian curses to recognize one when she heard it. "Bull," he ended in English.

"Watch your language in front of the baby," she chastised him, taking the little one from his arms, only to return her seconds later when the infant yodeled in protest at being taken from Michael's arms. Brett could empathize. She knew firsthand how incredibly good it felt to be in Michael's arms and how hard it was to leave his embrace.

"This is really weird," Michael noted. "I've never been any good with babies before. Whenever I got near one, they'd fuss and scream. Not that I've actually been around that many babies. I don't have any nephews or nieces. My younger sister and brother aren't even married yet, although a friend or two has had a baby... But enough about me. Let's get back to this bastard of a fiancé you had."

"He wasn't a bad person," Brett protested with a reprimanding look at his choice of word. "He took very good care of me after the operation."

"And dumped you after that."

"Not dumped. Let me down gently."

"And broke your heart in the process."

"Now you're being dramatic."

"It's my Rom blood."

She smiled at his wry words.

"That's better," he noted approvingly. "Now tell me what we're going to do with this baby."

"Maybe if you sit with her on the couch, she'll fall asleep," Brett suggested.

He nodded his agreement. "Sounds like a plan. Do you have a couch? I didn't notice one when you first moved in."

"Well, actually it's a daybed but it works as a couch." She pointed to the piece of furniture, with its calico-heart quilt and blue pillows. Passing by the scarred pine table on his way over there, he noticed all the baby paraphernalia she had piled on top of it.

Seeing his gaze, she said, "I don't suppose you have much experience changing diapers?"

"No." He looked as if she'd asked him if he'd ever performed brain surgery.

"Me neither. I'm hoping Tyrone can give me some pointers when he gets home from the hospital in the morning."

"Why would he give you pointers?"

"He's a nurse."

"On the psychiatric ward. Didn't he tell you that?"

"I haven't actually gotten to talk to him directly yet," Brett admitted. "Mostly I speak to his wife, Keisha. The psychiatric ward, huh?"

Michael nodded. "We may need to check ourselves in," he noted ruefully. "You do know what you're considering is crazy, don't you?"

"What am I considering?"

"Keeping this baby."

"The mother asked me to take care of her."

"For how long? And what if the mother comes back?"

"Then I'd give her baby back, of course. Providing she's able to take care of it properly."

"What kind of mother could abandon a baby?"

"One who knew she couldn't take care of it anymore."

"Then why didn't she drop it off at an adoption center or orphanage or something?"

"Because it might have been too hard to go through with it then. Maybe she had to do it quickly."

"Why pick the foyer of this building?"

"I've been thinking about that."

"And what did you come up with?"

"That the mother might know me. I work with a lot of kids at the youth center. They know I was a foster child. They also know that they can depend on me to help them out if they get into trouble."

"So you think one of those kids left their baby for you? But they're practically babies themselves."

"Old enough to get pregnant. One of the girls who helped me move in here had a baby last year."

"Wait a minute. There was a *girl* helping you move? I thought those kids were all boys."

"With the grunge look it can be a little hard to tell sometimes," Brett acknowledged dryly.

"But you're sure this baby is a girl?"

"Absolutely. I've had to change her diaper a couple of times already. I think I'm getting better at it. This time the diaper actually stayed on. The first few times she wormed and squiggled right out of it. And the directions on the box aren't much help. I've seen better directions on a faucet."

"Speaking of faucets, I think she's wet."

"Oh-oh."

"Here." Michael automatically went to hand the baby back to Brett, but the infant had other ideas—grabbing onto Michael's T-shirt and crying.

"You're clearly going to have to help me change her," Brett said. "She won't let you leave her."

"Usually when I have that effect on females, they're a little older," Michael noted ruefully. "But even then, it's nothing like this."

"Bring her over here to the table and then lay her down... that's it. Now keep her busy while I change her."

"Did the note say what her name was?"

"No."

"You can't just keep calling her 'Baby.' "

"I thought I'd call her Hope."

The little girl let out a gurgle as if confirming Brett's choice. "Sounds like she likes it," Michael said. "Isn't that right, Hope?" He shook a little rattly teddy bear that Brett had sitting on the table. The baby reached out and gurgled in delight. "Look, she smiled at me. Is she old enough to do that?"

"Obviously she is."

"How old do you think she is? Did the note say?"

"No, the note didn't say anything other than what I told you. As to Hope's age, I'm no expert, but I did buy a book while I was out. According to her weight, I'd say she's probably about six months old."

"Did you see how blue her eyes are?" Michael asked as he stared into the baby's face.

"She's gorgeous, isn't she? Although I confess that at the moment, you've got the better view," she noted dryly, removing the wet diaper.

"You've got that right," he agreed with a grin.

Her eyes were caught by his. The ensuing jolt of electricity that shot through her was a familiar one. She'd felt it when, as a ten-year-old, she'd tried to fix a broken light switch without first turning off the electricity at the junction box. She hadn't felt it again until the first day she'd met Michael. Now she experienced it each time they were together. At some point their eyes would meet, communicating in a visual shorthand that was heavy with anticipation and hot with dark promises.

This time, their visual communication was disrupted by the gurgling of the baby, who scooted sideways to get their attention.

Flustered, Brett looked down. "I...ahh...I didn't think it would be this hard diapering a baby. Look at how she moves around. She almost kicked me in the eye earlier when I was trying to figure out how the sticky tape fastened on the sides of these dumb diapers."

"Maybe she'll be a kick boxer when she grows up," Michael said. "How 'bout it, Hope? Is that one of your career goals?" The baby squealed and waved her hand, almost smacking him in the eye. "Hey, she's got a great right hook."

"There," Brett said, patting the fastening tape into place. "That should work." She added a prayer just in case. "Hope doesn't look sleepy anymore, does she?" It was more a resigned observation than a question.

"Maybe she's hungry? What have you fed her?"

"She drank apple juice and formula, but wouldn't eat much. I did buy baby food but she wasn't very interested in it. I sampled some of the apricot with tapioca myself and I have to say, it wasn't half-bad."

"Maybe we should put her in the car seat and see if she'll eat something now."

"It's worth a try. Okay, Hope, for tonight's entree we have a selection of strained carrots and turkey with rice or creamed corn and beef with egg noodles," she said, reading the labels from the glass jars of baby food.

"If I were you, I'd go for the carrots and turkey," Michael advised Hope as he settled her in the seat and fastened the harness around her. "Look, she nodded at me. Smart move," he congratulated the baby, who was clinging to his finger. "I can't get over how much she seems to like me. There must have been something wrong with those other babies," he declared.

"Okay, here's dinner, Hope. Yummy." Brett held the spoon up to the baby's mouth, which was harder to do than it sounded since the baby was suddenly as slippery as an eel—trying to slide out of the car seat while turning her head from side to side. A second later, Hope put her hand smack dab in the spoonful of baby food. Strained carrots dripped from her little fingers as she immediately reached for Michael's chin. "Maybe she wants you to eat some first," Brett said.

"What do I look like, a food tester?" he demanded. When Hope's face screwed up as if she were about to cry, he relented. "Okay, okay, look, I'm eating it, too." At the first taste, he made a grimace.

"Oh, right," Brett mockingly congratulated him. "That's the way to make her want to eat some."

He took another spoonful, this time smiling as if it killed him, while saying "Yummy."

"It would help if you said it as if you meant it," Brett added as Hope continued to look unconvinced.

"Listen, kid, eat this food and you'll grow up to be smart and beautiful like Brett here," Michael declared.

The baby stared at him a moment before letting him put the spoonful in her mouth.

"Sure, she lets *you* feed her but won't let me do it. Do you think there's something about me she doesn't like?" Brett asked. "She was good all afternoon, but tonight she started crying and wouldn't stop. I got worried that she might be sick, but she didn't seem warm or anything."

At that moment, Hope leaned forward and held out her arms to Brett.

Delighted, Brett leaned down to kiss the baby, getting baby food on her own face in the process.

"I guess that answers your question," Michael noted. "She likes you just fine. Who wouldn't?"

"You didn't when I first met you," Brett reminded him as she wiped off the baby food with a paper towel.

"I wasn't in the best of moods," he admitted. "But that was my fault, nothing to do with you. You're a huge hit with the tenants, surely you know that?"

*But am I a hit with you?* That's what Brett wanted to know, but was afraid to ask.

Instead, she watched while Michael fed Hope. He looked adorable with baby food still on his chin. She loved the way he bit his lip while feeding the baby and had to laugh at the way he got into the assignment—right down to making propeller noises as he moved the spoon toward the little girl's mouth.

Seeing her look, he shrugged self-consciously. "My sister did that for our younger brother when he was a baby. He seemed to like it."

"So does Hope. I can't believe you thought you weren't good with babies."

"Trust me, this is definitely a first."

"Then I'm honored to be sharing it with you."

His answering smile warmed her clear down to her toes. In that moment it was easy to imagine that they were a family, that Hope was their baby and that Michael was her...

Stop right there, Brett ordered her thoughts. She'd never been the type to daydream like this before. Well, okay, as a kid she'd daydreamed that there was a family out there who'd want to adopt her. But that had passed by the time she was nine. Since then she'd always had her feet on the ground, in her own way. She and Bill had planned their future right down to how many years apart they'd have their children. But all those plans had gone down the toilet when fate had stepped in, depriving her of the ability to have babies of her own.

Brett had tried to accept reality, had focused her attention on helping others, had worked toward getting her degree in psychology. But deep down inside her there remained a cold darkness that had never gone away. Until Hope had come into her life that morning. When Brett held the little girl, she finally acknowledged how very much she'd still wanted to have a baby. It isn't fair, she'd raged inside... only to hear her calmer side saying *Since when is life supposed to be fair?*

"You've gone awfully quiet all of a sudden," Michael said. "You okay?"

"Sure. I was just thinking, that's all."

"About what?"

"Stuff."

"Ah, yes. Stuff." He nodded his head in teasing understanding. "I often think about stuff myself."

"You do?"

"Sure. Like how do they get the stripes into those striped toothpastes?"

She smiled at his attempt to cheer her up and got into the spirit of things. "Or bubbles in soda. How do those get in there?"

"What about neckties? Whose bright idea were those?"

"Or fireflies? Ever wonder how they light up that way?"

"And the phone. Why does it always ring when you're in the bathroom?"

"I know the answer to that one," Brett replied. "Murphy's Law. Whatever can go wrong, does."

"Not always."

"More often than not," she said with the matter-of-factness of someone who's had more things go wrong than right in her life. "There, Hope finished off the entire jar of baby food. Good girl!" Brett congratulated her with a kiss, which left the baby giggling.

"Okay, what's next?" Michael asked.

Brett paused, trying to remember if you were supposed to burp a six-month-old after they ate. Or was that only for younger babies? She'd tried burping Hope after feeding her the liquids. One thing she knew for sure, it was safer keeping a towel on her shoulder for emergencies. Since the little girl wasn't fussing, she opted for skipping the burping this time.

Another thought occurred to her. "Maybe she's having trouble sleeping because she's teething." Hope started fussing and waving her hands, clearly wanting out of the car seat.

"We better get her out of that thing before she starts screaming the building down again," Michael said, before undoing the harness and lifting the baby out.

"I couldn't get a good look in her mouth by myself, but maybe you could hold her while I look in her mouth with a flashlight."

"Hold her how?" he asked suspiciously.

"Just sit down on the rocking chair with her on your lap."

After doing as she suggested, he said, "And how do you propose to get her mouth open?"

"Her mouth is open more often than it's closed."

"Unless you're trying to feed her baby food."

"Which we're not." Brett retrieved a compact flashlight from her tool kit. "Okay, Hope. Open up, honey. I just want to check and see what you've got in there."

Thinking Brett was playing a game with her, Hope pulled her eel imitation again, squealing and squirming on Michael's lap, her legs and arms flying in all directions, making Michael very nervous as the baby's foot got dangerously close to his private parts. "Careful there, kid," he warned Hope. "You kick me any harder and I'm gonna be singing soprano."

"Maybe I should hold her and you can look in her mouth."

Michael eagerly took Brett up on her suggestion, before realizing he wasn't that keen to stick his fingers in a baby's mouth. "Does she bite?" he asked.

"Not if she doesn't have teeth."

"But what if she does?"

"I think front teeth are the last to come in."

"You *think?*"

"That's why we're looking in her mouth, to see if she has any teeth."

"What's with this *we* business? I'm the one putting my life on the line here," he grumbled good-naturedly.

"Hey, it's a wet job, but somebody's got to do it," she retorted. "While you're looking in her mouth, check to see if you see any redness."

Hope held still long enough for him to open her mouth and flash the light inside. "It's all red in here," he reported. "Mouths are supposed to be red."

"I meant bright red. Any sign of swelling?"

"I don't think so."

"Any teeth?"

"Yeah. One on the bottom. Part of one, anyway," he amended.

"That might be it, then. That must be why she's crying."

"She's not crying now."

"Because you're here. But you can't stay all night."

There was a pause, as if they were both tempted by the idea, before Brett launched into speech. "Maybe I should try rubbing her gums with a cloth wrapped around an ice cube. I read in the book I bought that it sometimes helps to ease the pain."

"Whose? The kid's or ours?" Michael inquired. "She's gnawing on my finger."

"Babies do that."

"Good thing she doesn't have more teeth. Messy, aren't you?" Michael observed as Hope drooled all over his hand.

"Sorry," Brett apologized, handing him a paper towel from the roll she'd brought with her to the rocking chair. "You could probably leave as soon as I apply the ice."

While Hope seemed to like having the cloth-wrapped ice rubbed on her gums, she showed no sign of settling down for the night. And when the baby saw Michael heading for the door, she let out a cry that made both adults wince.

"She really seems to have formed an attachment to you," Brett said.

"I have that affect on females," Michael said with a tired grin.

"Look, maybe if you tried lying down with her on the daybed, she'll nod off."

"If *she* doesn't, I might," Michael ruefully acknowledged.

"I'm sorry about this," Brett murmured.

"Don't be. It's been . . . quite an experience."

"It isn't over yet," she reminded him before fixing the bed, removing the largest decorative pillows so that it would be more comfortable.

"Now I know why you decided to call her Hope," Michael said. "Because you *hope* she's going to sleep through the night."

"The night is already half over."

"What if I roll over and squish her or something?" he asked, his earlier trepidation returning as he gingerly sat on the bed.

"Here, maybe just kinda of lean against these pillows...." Putting a hand on his shoulder, she moved him forward and tucked the decorative pillows back behind him so that he was at a forty-five-degree angle. "How's that?" she asked. "Comfy?"

"Oh sure. Don't I look comfy?"

"Not really."

"I've got a better idea. Get all the pillows out of the way, and you and I lie down with the baby between us. That way she can't escape."

Trouble was, Brett wouldn't be able to escape either—escape the temptation of being so close to him. "I don't think that's a good idea," she said.

"Why not? Are you scared? You? The woman who can fix water heaters with a mere flick of her wrist? What can happen with a baby between us? She's got to be better protection than a chastity belt," he stated dryly. "Besides, I think she's exhausted us both too much to be amorous." Seeing her weakening, he held out his hand to her. "Come on. Try it. You'll like it."

"Yeah, that's what I'm afraid of," she muttered, even as she put her hand in his. The electricity was still there, but this time there was an accompanying sense of comfort. Working together, they got rid of the superfluous pillows and stretched out on what was after all just a twin mattress. The logistics were tricky at first, but they managed.

Propping her head on one elbow, Brett watched Hope closely as the baby examined her new situation.

"A watched baby never sleeps," Michael told her.

"I think she's looking a little sleepy," Brett said. "Sorry," she added for his benefit as her bare foot bumped into his leg.

Half sitting up, he reached for her denim-clad knee and draped her leg over his. "There, that's better."

"Know any lullabies?" she asked in a breathless whisper. Her leg still hummed where he'd touched it, and this new proximity was provocatively intimate. Despite it all, Brett resolutely kept her attention fixed on Hope, who actually yawned. Next thing Brett knew, she was yawning, too. Michael's yawn was a second behind.

They shared a sheepish grin. "I guess it's true that yawning is contagious after all," he said.

"What about that lullaby?"

"I only know part of one."

"Fine. I've exhausted my repertoires on her—from 'Rockaby Baby' to 'Crocodile Rock.' Nothing worked."

"Let's try this...."

He started softly singing what she guessed to be a Hungarian lullaby, since the words and melody were unfamiliar to her. Hope was fascinated. So was Brett. Before dozing off, she sternly reminded herself that under no circumstances was she to pretend that she'd finally gotten her Christmas wish—a family of her own. It was only make-believe....

Michael woke at the crack of dawn with the mother of all backaches. After opening his eyes, it took him a moment or two to remember where he was. Little Hope was still out like a light. So was Brett. Both looked adorable, but he was going to get a charley horse in his leg if he didn't move right now.

Easing away, he managed to get out of bed without waking either of them, and without doing himself any further bodily harm. Luckily he'd ended up on the outside edge of the bed.

He felt like he'd been pulled through a knothole backward. Running a hand over his face, he felt the raspiness of a night's worth of stubble. A shower and a shave sounded like heaven about now. Not wanting to wake them, he tiptoed over to the door and quietly unlocked it. Giving the sleeping woman and child one more look to make sure all was well, Michael backed out the door.

"Why, Mr. Janos!" Consuela Martinez exclaimed from the hallway. "Whatever are you doing sneaking out of Brett's apartment at this early hour of the morning?"

# Five

Startled, Michael groggily blinked at the woman. "Sneaking? I wasn't sneaking. What are you doing down here?"

"I came down to do the wash. The question is, what are *you* doing down here? Not that I need an answer. I may be on Social Security, but I've got 20/20 vision. So you and Brett are...seeing each other, huh? I knew the two of you were meant for each other that very first day. I have second sight about these things, you know."

Great, Michael grimly thought to himself. First he was receiving Rom magic boxes in the mail, now he had a tenant who claimed she had second sight. "It's not what you think," he began.

"I hope you plan on making an honest woman of Brett," Mrs. Martinez interrupted him to say reprimandingly. "She's a good girl. Does a lot at the church. You shouldn't take advantage of your position as her boss to go having hanky-panky."

"He didn't take advantage of me, Consuela," Brett inserted from behind him. "If anything, *I* took advantage of *him.*"

The older woman blinked in surprise. "Well, I must say you girls are bolder than we used to be."

"He helped me with a baby I'm taking care of," Brett explained.

"A baby? Where?" She leaned past them to look into Brett's apartment, her gaze zooming in on the sleeping baby. "Oh, isn't she adorable! What's her name?"

"Hope."

"I didn't know you had a baby," Consuela said.

"No, I'm just taking care of her for a while," Brett replied.

"Is she going to be staying long?"

"Could be," Brett returned.

"Where is her crib?"

Doing some quick thinking, Brett said, "Uh, my friend didn't bring it with her."

"Don't worry, with ten grandchildren I've got access to plenty of baby stuff." Consuela began listing some items that would be needed. "I can get you a crib, a playpen and you'll need some more clothes I'll bet . . . oh, my daughter has the cutest little dresses from when her daughter was little. And one of those bounce chairs would be perfect for Hope. I'll go on upstairs and start calling around to get these things."

"Thanks. You're a real sweetie!" Brett gave her a hug.

"Why didn't you tell her about finding Hope in the foyer?" Michael asked Brett after the older woman had left.

"Because I didn't want her to go to the authorities. The fewer people who know about the true circumstances of what happened, the better. I already risked suspicion by asking the tenants if they'd had any visitors with a baby yesterday. I don't think they'll make the connection, though.''

"You know, it occurred to me that we do need to make sure that this baby wasn't kidnapped or something."

"Kidnapped! What makes you think that?"

"It could be a possibility. Look, I've got some connections at the police department from my academy days."

"You went to the police academy?"

"Actually I dropped out. I guess you could say that I don't take orders well."

"That I can believe," she noted wryly. "Are you sure you can make inquiries without tipping the authorities off that she was abandoned?"

"Trust me on this, okay? We just need to make sure that her parents aren't out there desperately looking for her."

"But the note..."

"Could have been something to draw people off the trail. I don't think we'll find that Hope has been kidnapped, but I'd feel better if we made sure, wouldn't you?"

"I guess so."

"Okay, so that's what we'll do.'

It hadn't gone unnoticed by her that he was using the term *we*. Each time he said it, another inch of her heart melted.

"I know her eyes are blue and her hair is dark and you think she's six or seven months old. What about any identifiable marks?" Michael asked.

"She's got a rose-colored birthmark on her bottom that's sort of shaped like a flower. It's on her left side. I noticed it when I was diapering her."

"Okay, I'll include that in the description I'll give my contact down at police headquarters. Oh-oh, she's awake," Michael noted, as he scooped up the fussing baby. "Do you need help giving her breakfast?" he asked.

"That's okay. You're going to be late for work."

"I've got time yet."

"Well, then, yes, I could use some help. Thanks. I'll just change her diapers first and if you could pick out a jar of baby food for breakfast..."

But once Hope was cleaned up and settled in the car seat, the baby decided to stop being so cooperative. She let Michael give her one spoonful of food, only to blow bubbles with the next spoonful instead of swallowing it.

"Geez, I've seen sloppy eaters in my day, kid, but you take the cake."

The little girl giggled with delight.

"It wasn't meant to be a compliment," Michael told her. "Now eat this. Yummy. See, I'm eating some. Now you eat some."

Hope grabbed the spoon before he got it to her mouth, and sent it flying across the room. Determined not to be outwitted by a six-month-old, Michael retrieved the spoon and tried again. Hope smiled angelically at him and ate the next spoonful.

"That's better," he said approvingly. "Good girl. Now here comes another planeful of goodies...." He waved the spoon toward her mouth.

This time the baby reached for the food on the spoon and then threw it at him. "You're supposed to eat the food, not wear it in your hair," Brett said, having just returned from a trip to the bathroom.

"I think it takes two people to feed this kid," he decided.

Half an hour later, Brett stared at the surrounding chaos in exhausted dismay. The experience had left both adults looking as if they'd taken part in a college-dorm food fight.

"Who'd have thought feeding one baby could create such havoc?" Michael said wearily.

"At least she didn't do this last night when we gave her strained carrots. That would be harder to get off the walls than apple sauce."

"What does that book you got say about feedings?"

Brett wiped baby food from the paperback book before opening it up and checking the index. "It says a rain slicker might be useful garb."

"For the baby or for us?"

"Both, maybe," she replied. "Yuck, I need to take a shower."

"So do I."

Their eyes met. The thought of sharing a shower with Michael filled her head with steamy thoughts as she imagined the individual droplets of water slowly trailing down his bare body—past his collarbone, down his chest to his navel and below....

It wasn't even seven in the morning and already she was having X-rated fantasies about the man!

"I...uh...you didn't get much sleep last night," Brett noted breathlessly with that stuttering start she seemed to have acquired since meeting Michael. "Are you sure you'll be okay to go to work today?"

"Sure. I'm a little stiff...." His voice trailed off as another kind of stiffness came to mind. Looking at her now, he thought she was sexy as hell, with her dark hair fluffed and falling into her big blue eyes.

"You go take your shower and I'll watch the baby," Michael told her.

"Thanks. I won't be long."

As she hurried off, Michael studied the baby, who was contentedly babbling to herself. The kid was cute, even if she was a menace at feeding time. Hope's big blue eyes reminded him of Brett's. No wonder she'd been so drawn to the baby—not that she wouldn't have been drawn to any infant in need. Or adult for that matter.

Out of curiosity, Michael had stopped by St. Gerald's Youth Center a few days ago and he'd gotten an earful about all the help she'd been—there and at the homeless shelter affiliated with the same charity. Brett was one of the rare ones who gave of themselves, trying to make the world a better place for those around her, seeing them as individuals, working with them one-on-one. The priest had told him that Brett's God-given strength was making people feel at ease with her. "She doesn't see social problems, she sees people," Father Lyden had said. "People who need her help. So she's there for them. I only wish we had more like her, but then Brett is pretty much one of a kind."

Watching her as she came out of the bathroom fresh from her shower, her hair still wet, her creamy skin flushed as she finished tying the belt on her pink terry-cloth robe, Michael had to agree that Brett was indeed one of a kind.

"You're looking at me funny again. What's the matter? Do I still have baby food on my face?" Brett asked him.

"No. I just like looking at you."

Her heart did a complete backward somersault. "You do?"

He nodded. "Think you can get used to it?"

She nodded.

Reaching out to brush his knuckles against her flushed cheek, he said, "I'll call you later, after I've checked with the police, okay?"

"Okay."

And then he was gone, but the lingering effect of his words and his touch stayed with her throughout the day.

Brett finished replacing the light fixture in the Stephanopolises dining room while Hope happily watched from the bounce chair provided by Consuela's oldest daughter.

Mrs. Stephanopolis was delighted at having the baby in her apartment and didn't want them to leave even after the new fixture was in place and the electricity turned back on at the junction box. "Stay for some tea. You never did tell me where you learned Greek," she added.

"I took some classes in college. And I knew a few words before.... One of my favorite foster moms ran a group home and she was Greek. She made the best cookies at Christmas... with raisins and cinnamon. I was only there one year, though."

"You had no relatives who could take you in?"

Brett shook her head before sipping the tea she'd been given. She and Mrs. Stephanopolis talked for a few moments before Brett gathered Hope and the bounce chair and made her way downstairs to her own place.

Brett walked into her apartment to hear the phone ringing. After setting Hope into the playpen that Consuela had provided, she grabbed the phone. "Hello?"

"It's Michael. My contact at the police department has done some preliminary checking and so far so good. No reports of a kidnapped baby matching her description."

"Thank heavens for that." She sighed in relief.

"He's going to check the out-of-state reports, just to make sure, and get back to me tomorrow."

"Are you sure he won't say anything?"

"I'm sure. Listen I've got to go," he said. "I'll see you later."

When Michael got home that evening, he immediately cocked his head to listen for any sign of Hope crying. All was quiet from the basement. Thumbing through his mail, he saw a postcard from his brother Dylan. The card had been sent from Oklahoma but that didn't mean his brother was still there. As the rolling stone in the family, Dylan was rarely in one place for long. But he usually made a point of staying in touch, although not as often as their parents might have liked.

Michael had no sooner sat down in his recliner when the phone rang. He hoped it might be his dad calling back with more information about the Rom box, but instead it was his sister. "Listen, Gaylynn, did Dad ever mention anything to you about a family curse?"

"I thought you didn't believe in any of the Gypsy superstitions," she countered.

"I don't. I'm just curious."

"How come?"

"I got a package in the mail from some great-aunt or something in Hungary."

"Cool. What is it?"

"A box."

"A magical box! I can't wait to see it."

"Wait a second—I never said it was magic."

"You're asking me about family curses. And if the box came from Dad's side of the family, there's bound to be magic involved."

"So did Dad tell you anything about a curse or not?"

"Not to do with a box, no. He did tell me that seeing a spider in my bedroom at night is good luck."

"That's not very helpful."

"Mom and Dad will be back from their cruise before you know it. You'll just have to wait until then. I was calling to see if you were going to pick them up at the airport or if I should."

"Why don't you go ahead and do that? I may be tied up."

"With what? Are you working on a new case?"

"In a manner of speaking."

"It's a woman," his sister guessed. "Are you seeing some blonde bimbette?"

"No. She's got dark hair and she knows her way around a toolbox better than I do."

"I think I'm going to like her," Gaylynn said. "So, when do I get to meet her?"

"I don't know. Maybe during the holidays. Listen, I've got to go. Talk to you again soon. Take care, kiddo."

After hanging up, Michael decided that it sounded entirely too quiet downstairs. He'd better go down just to make sure everything was okay.

When he got outside Brett's door he could hear the sound of shrieks. Knocking on the door, he said, "Are you okay in there?"

"Come on in, it's unlocked."

"What are you doing leaving the door unlocked?" he demanded as he walked inside. "This is Chicago, for God's sake. Do you know how many murders take place in this city every year?"

"Calm down. I just unlocked it two minutes ago when I heard you coming down the stairs."

"What are you doing?"

"Giving Hope a bath. Or trying to, anyway," she muttered as the little one squirmed away. "The thing is, it takes ten hands to hold her. You think she was slippery before, you should try her when she's all soapy."

"Want me to help?"

"Yes. Here, hold her while I try and wash her."

"If she's the one taking the bath, how come *you're* all wet?"

"You'll see."

A second later he did, as Hope gleefully smacked her hands, palm down, on the water—splashing it right in his face and then gurgling at him.

"Oh, so you think that's funny, do you? Well listen, little girl, the object here is for you to get wet. Not Brett and me."

"That's right. You tell her," Brett said with a grin.

"Look how cute her fingernails are. I didn't notice them last night. Hey, she's got toenails, too."

"Of course she does. Today I discovered that she loves to play peek-a-boo with me."

"I'd love to play peek-a-boo with you, too," he murmured with a wicked grin.

Her breath caught as she was captivated by the way his eyes crinkled at the corners when he smiled. His angular face was more often serious than not. Seeing the devilish upward tilt of his lips... the expression of seductive humor...was like stumbling upon an unexpected pot of gold.

The interlude was interrupted by the baby splashing water in Brett's face. Hope also got Brett's T-shirt, which now clung to her like those in a wet T-shirt competition. Looking down, Brett was embarrassed to see her nipples standing out against the material plastered against her skin. Her face grew even more flushed as she realized that Michael was staring at her with clear male appreciation.

"Here, you watch Hope for a minute," she muttered before grabbing a flannel shirt from the back of the chair and yanking it on. "We'd better take her out of the bathwater now, before she turns into a prune," she said, feeling like a prudish prune herself for making such a big deal over a little water on her T-shirt. It wasn't as if she was well endowed and had a lot to show off.

While Brett powdered and diapered the baby, Michael played This Little Pig Went to Market with Hope, wiggling each of the little girl's bare toes as he made up his own football-related verses. "This little piggy kicked a field goal. This one got an interception. This little piggy got a sack and, oh no, this little piggie fumbled the ball! But look, this little piggy got a punt return and scored a touchdown for the Bears."

Brett blew her bangs out of her eyes, feeling all thumbs due to Michael's close proximity.

Seeing the trouble she was having, Michael said, "Want me to do that?"

Brett nodded and stepped aside.

When he tried to get Hope into the pink terry-cloth sleeper, he was amazed that she still had enough energy to wiggle like an eel. "This is harder than tackling the 49ers leading receiver," he muttered as the baby got away from him yet again. When he finally got the snaps done up on her sleeper, he lifted the little girl and triumphantly said, "All done."

"And she looks very nice," Brett teasingly congratulated him. "Except for the fact that her legs aren't in the sleeper."

Looking more closely he realized that, sure enough, he'd fastened the snaps incorrectly. "It's humbling to be outwitted by a six-month-old," he noted ruefully.

"Tell me about it. It's a good thing I don't have much furniture, because she's starting to creep and sort of crawl. I had to pull her out from under the table half a dozen times before I put her back in the playpen."

"I wish I'd seen her crawling."

"She can even look backward by lifting her little fanny and looking under her tummy to see where she's been. It's a sight. I took a couple of pictures of her doing that. Okay, I took an entire roll. I'll show them to you when I get them developed. You were adorable, weren't you, Hope?"

The little girl yawned. A second later Michael did, too.

"You're tired," Brett said. "You should go on home and get some rest. I can put her to bed."

But Hope had other ideas. As soon as Michael got to the door she let out a cry that made both adults wince.

"Maybe if you just sat in the rocking chair and rocked her until she drops off to sleep..." Brett hesitantly suggested.

"It's worth a try," Michael agreed. Fifteen minutes later, both he and the baby were asleep. Looking at them, Brett was struck by what an endearing picture they made. The little baby's hand lay so trustingly on his broad chest. His big hand cupped Hope protectively. But she couldn't let Michael sleep in her rocking chair indefinitely, or he'd wake up with one heck of a crick in his neck.

Moving carefully, Brett picked up the sleeping infant, sighing with relief when she didn't wake up, even after

Brett put her down in the crib. Now she had to wake Michael. She gently put her hand on his shoulder. A second later, he leapt to his feet, every muscle in his body alert like a soldier ready for dangerous action.

Startled, Brett jumped back.

"Sorry," he muttered, running his hand through his hair.

"That's okay. I didn't mean to startle you."

"Where's Hope?"

"In bed. Which is where you should be. In your own bed. You need the rest."

What he needed was Brett, in *his* bed, and that erotic image stayed with Michael throughout the long night.

The next day, Thursday, was a repeat of the one before, with Brett doing more repairs on the building while Hope bounced happily in her chair.

Michael stopped by right after dinner. "I heard from my friend at the police department today," he told her. "He checked the out-of-state reports and there's no indication that Hope was kidnapped."

"I told you so," she replied.

"Have you thought any more about your plans?"

"Plans?"

"For the future. For Hope."

"I don't know."

"You have to have a plan, Brett. Babies need stuff. Like Social Security numbers. She's going to need one by the time she's a year old, you know."

"You're kidding me."

"I'm not."

"I can't worry that far ahead. I'm taking things one day at a time."

Michael checked in with Brett again after work on Friday. This time when she opened the door she looked dressed up. Not in sequins and spangles or anything like

that. But the sweater she had on was a festive one with
Santa on the front. And she wore lipstick, something she
rarely did, not that her lush lips needed artificial coloring.
Then he remembered that this was a Friday night. "Going
out on a date or something?"

"Bite your tongue," she murmured with a grin. "Nope.
The Christmas tree-trimming party at St. Gerald's Youth
Center is tonight. I was just getting ready to leave. I made
cookies to bring along."

"I thought I smelled something good."

"You're welcome to come if you'd like. If you don't
have anything else to do, I mean. But you probably do,
right? I mean, the holidays are a real busy time for people, I know that."

"I'm not doing anything tonight. Aside from accompanying you and Hope to the Christmas party. Providing
I don't have to do anything weird like dress up as Santa."

"No, nothing weird."

"Okay, then I'd like to go with you. Are you ready to go
now?"

"Just about, yes." Brett hurriedly checked her appear-
ance in the mirror by the front door. She'd originally
planned on wearing her dangling green ornament earrings
tonight. But when Hope had started pulling on them,
nearly ripping her ear off in the process, Brett had decided that might not be such a good idea, after all. Instead she put in a pair of sterling-silver stud earrings
shaped like Christmas trees. At least her hair was short, so
the baby couldn't really pull on that much. She was quickly
learning that dark clothes showed the stains less than
lighter ones did, which made her black leggings and red
sweater the perfect attire.

"Would you rather carry the cookies or the baby?" she
asked Michael.

"I'd better carry Hope or I might be tempted to eat half
the cookies."

"I saved a bunch for you. I wasn't sure if you liked them."

"Who doesn't like chocolate-chip cookies? Here, give me that," he said as she tried to juggle the baby bag over one shoulder. "I've got broader shoulders than you do."

"Yeah, I noticed," she murmured as she followed him outside. She also noticed the confident way he held Hope, who was bundled up in a snowsuit. "You're getting very good at that," Brett said.

"Yeah, I guess I am. Pretty amazing, huh?"

"Yeah," she agreed softly, thinking what a perfect picture he made holding the little girl. He'd be a great father, protective and caring.

They drove in Michael's car. Hope, who was fastened in her car seat, was in the back seat with Brett, who kept her amused with a toy during the short ride. Brett thought the baby looked lost in the snowsuit that Consuela had lent her. She'd grow into it in another three months or so.

At least the weather wasn't bad for driving. There was hardly any snow left from the inch or two they'd gotten a few days before. In fact, the forecasters were predicting very mild weather for the next few days.

The youth center was already busy when they arrived. Michael managed to snare the last empty chair for Brett. She smiled at his courtly gesture, not that she planned on doing much sitting. There was too much to do.

But first she held Hope and carefully removed the too-big snowsuit from the little one.

"You sure there's a baby in there?" Michael teasingly asked. "Ah, there she is. Gorgeous as ever."

"Me or the baby?" Brett retorted with a grin.

"Both of you."

Her fingers brushed his as they both reached for Hope. Brett froze, the surrounding noise fading into the distance as the sound of her own heart beating filled her ears. And all because Michael was stroking the back of her hand with

his fingertips, caressing her with persuasive gentleness.
He'd turned what had started as an accidental touch into
a seductive exploration. It was almost frightening how
many sparks were generated by such a simple action. The
moment was interrupted by Hope drooling on them. Startled back into their surroundings, Brett had to laugh. Talk
about dampening the fires of passion.

He just touched your hand, she reminded herself. Don't
go all adolescent.

Focusing her attention on Hope, Brett watched her
closely, to see if all the surrounding mayhem was bother-
ing the baby. Christmas music blared from a boombox in
one corner and the room was filled with people. But Hope
looked happy to be there.

Within seconds, a group of kids and teenagers flocked
around, immediately noticing the bundle in Brett's arms.
"Hey, where'd you get that baby?"

"I'm watching her for a friend."

A dozen more questions followed. Michael noticed how
patiently Brett answered them all. The next thing he noticed was the pair of sad-looking Christmas trees drunk-
enly leaning in the corner.

The short tree seemed to be reserved for the younger
kids to decorate as they chose. Michael was itching to un-
tangle the mess they'd made of the lights, which looked
like they'd been tossed onto the tree to land where they
may. As if reading his mind, Brett said, "It's their tree to
decorate as they like. Gets it out of their system. The larger
tree will be more traditional—sort of."

The younger kids had made their own ornaments—out
of everything from aluminum foil to the cups from egg
cartons—with their names on them. Picking a place to
hang the special keepsakes resulted in a few arguments,
which Brett was adept at resolving. She managed to jiggle
Hope on her hip, supervise the cookies being set out on the
table and sign her name to a huge homemade card for

Santa Claus all at the same time. Michael was amazed. But then he'd been amazed from the very first day he'd met her.

Seeing him looking at her, she smiled and waved him over. "Can you hold Hope for a while?" she asked him. "I've got to make sure they didn't use too many extension cords when they hooked up the tree lights."

"Sure. No problem."

And so Michael found himself sitting in the chair he'd originally snagged for Brett, playing horsie with Hope on his knee. She had the cutest giggle. Hearing it warmed his heart.

Seeing Brett bent over beneath the tree did more than just warm his heart. She set fire to various parts of his anatomy. The past two nights he'd seen her in his dreams, made love to her, kissed every inch of bare skin, searched every curve for hidden freckles.

His steamy thoughts were interrupted by Juan's grinning face blocking Michael's view of Brett. "You don't look lonely no more," the teenager noted. "Brett's been working her magic on you, for sure."

"I guess you could say that," Michael agreed.

Juan's use of the word magic got Michael to thinking about the Rom box again. His parents would be home a few days before Christmas. He'd have to wait until then to find out the details about the spell or curse or whatever it was. He was sure they'd fall hard for the baby.

Watching the little girl's face light up as she gurgled and babbled at him, Michael realized that he was getting to be as bad as Brett, thinking of the baby as his. Feeling something damp on his knee, he realized something else.

"Hope Springs Eternal," he murmured to Brett as she rejoined him.

"Don't I know it," she agreed, wondering if he'd noticed the surreptitious looks she'd been giving him from across the room.

"I meant the baby. She's wet . . . again."

"I'll take care of it," Brett said, grabbing the diaper bag and Hope.

"Taking care of things is Brett's specialty," Father Lyden noted as he sat on the chair on Michael's other side. "She seems very attached to her friend's baby."

Sensing an underlying meaning in the priest's comment, Michael said, "Is there something wrong with that?"

"There is if the baby is only staying with her temporarily. It may be hard for Brett when her friend returns."

"It's not certain that her friend will ever return. It's a complicated situation," Michael said, his upbringing making him uncomfortable with lying to a priest.

"I just don't want to see Brett hurt. She's done so much for others. She deserves some happiness for herself. She's the one who organized the toy drive so that the children could receive presents tonight. Ah, I see she's coming back to you now. I suppose I'd better start seeing about distributing those presents."

For the next half hour the excitement and noise level rose as the presents were handed out.

"You know, when I was a kid," Michael said, "my family had a holiday tradition for St. Nicolas's Day on December 6th. We'd put our boots on the windowsill and if we'd been good, Télapó—that's the Hungarian Santa Claus—would fill the boot with goodies. We'd find tangerines, apples, and walnuts . . . although one year Télapó did leave football playing cards for me along with some bubblegum."

"I love to hear about traditions like that. So many countries have special contributions of their own. Just look around this room." She waved her hand. A majority of the kids were African-American and Hispanic but there were also some Asian kids there, too. "Different ethnic backgrounds, different traditions."

"It's a regular melting pot," Michael said.

She nodded. "Christmas seems to bring everyone together. It's one of the reasons why it's my favorite holiday."

"And the other reason?"

"The magic."

"Ah, yes. Magic." Michael had never been one to believe in it before, but seeing the glow in Brett's eyes he felt something unfolding in his heart. Looking at Hope, he was surprised to see the little girl was sound asleep.

"Maybe the secret is to make a lot of noise and then she'll fall asleep," Michael whispered to Brett.

"It's getting late," she whispered back. "We should take her home."

Home. For the first time the concept didn't scare him. Even visions of chintz couches couldn't make him uneasy.

"Let me just get those cookies I made for you," Brett said after they'd arrived back at her apartment. She'd already put Hope, who was still sound asleep, down for the night. Since then she'd been hovering like a jittery hummingbird. "Would you like some coffee?"

Putting his hand on her arm to anchor her in one place, he murmured, "What I'd like is this...."

Without further ado, he kissed her.

The moment had been building for some time, since their last kiss, their very first kiss. Where before Brett had felt as if she'd been engulfed in flames when his mouth had touched hers, now it was more like being totally immersed in something devilishly delicious and totally irresistible. Michael began slowly, as if they had all the time in the world to explore and enjoy. Brushing his lips back and forth against hers created a friction that Brett found delightful.

Preoccupied with the enchanting feel of his mouth moving against hers, she didn't even notice that she'd parted her lips until the kiss moved on to the next step. The wild singing in her bloodstream was echoed in the reckless chant of her heartbeat. Closing her eyes, she shut out the rest of the world, her entire focus centered on the beckoning pleasure. He awakened her senses to the simple glory of the roughly murmured sound of him whispering her name, the warmth of his fingers threading through her hair, the clean smell of his skin.

He shifted his hands so that they gently cupped the back of her head as their kiss deepened, his tongue stroking hers with passionate familiarity. Looping her arms around his neck, Brett leaned closer and let herself go.

Her reward was his husky growl of approval as he slid his hands down her back, tugging her into his heated embrace. Her breasts brushed against his chest with every breath either of them took. Excitement made her breathe even faster as he lifted his mouth only to shift and lower it for a kiss that was utterly consuming. He experimented with angles and tickling nibbles. She responded with creative moves of her own.

When his hands finally moved to the bare skin beneath her sweater, she almost wept with relief. She didn't want the barrier of clothing between them. With the first touch of his hand trailing up her back she knew she'd been waiting for this moment all her life.

They fit together like a lock and key. His hands caressed her with gentle fierceness, every sliding move creating sparks that lit her soul.

Twining her fingers in his hair, she gasped as he finally undid the fastening on her bra only to steal beneath its silky contours and brush the soft underside of her breasts with his fingertips. Feeling her melting response, he grew bolder, shoving her bra out of the way in order to cover her breasts with his hands. Her nipples grazed his palms as he handled her with heavenly skill, his touch evoking an intimacy that was both powerful and poignant.

The closeness of their embrace left her in no doubt as to the urgency of his needs. Her own needs were clamoring for satisfaction when the sound of a baby crying shattered her concentration.

Brett felt Michael trembling as he buried his face in her hair, his fingers clenched against her shoulders as he sought to regain control.

Moments later, Brett was free.

Feeling like a sleepwalker who'd just been jolted awake, Brett automatically made her way over to the crib to soothe the crying little girl. "It's all right, baby," she whispered, as much for her own benefit as Hope's. "It'll be okay."

But would it be? Even as Brett rocked Hope in her arms, her mind was scrambling to deal with what had just happened. This time she hadn't been the only one affected by the kiss she'd shared with Michael. This time it had been so much more than a kiss!

Michael watched her, knowing that if the baby hadn't interrupted them they might well have ended up...where? Where was this heading? When she was in his arms he couldn't think straight. He'd never felt such raw need for a woman before. He wanted her, it was that simple.

When his pager went off, Michael checked it before gruffly asking Brett, "Can I use your phone?"

"Sure."

Michael watched Brett put Hope back in her crib while he impatiently waited to be connected to his contact at the police department. "Janos here," he said curtly. "What's up?"

"Bad news."

"The baby? Was it kidnapped after all?"

"No, but it may soon be. From your friend."

"What are you talking about?"

"I don't know how she heard, I swear I didn't tell her. She must have heard me talking on the phone to you."

"Who?"

"The social worker from hell."

"A social worker knows about the baby?" Michael swore.

"I'm sorry, man. I thought I should warn you just in case she starts snooping around. I don't think she has your address, but she probably heard me saying your name. Maybe she won't follow up, she's got a work load big enough for a dozen people. But she's been bugging me for more info about this 'mystery baby,' as she calls it."

"Keep putting her off. The baby is fine. We're going to be adopting her."

"Don't you have to be married to do that?"

"We will be. Thanks for the warning."

After hanging up, Michael turned to find Brett standing behind him. "That was your friend at the police station, wasn't it. What did he say?"

"Too much."

"Is something wrong?"

"Nothing we can't fix by getting married."

# Six

"Married?" she gulped.

"That's right. It's the sensible thing to do."

"That's not the way marriage is usually described."

"That's because most people make the mistake of getting all wrapped up in emotion and don't use their heads."

Wrapped up in emotion? Brett thought to herself in dismay. She'd practically been drowning in it when he'd held her a few minutes ago.

"I can't imagine why your head would be telling you that marrying me would be a sensible thing to do," she said. "You don't even know me that well."

"I know you better than you think."

She didn't challenge him on that statement. How could she, when she felt the same way about him? As if she'd known him before, in another time or another life.

"What did your friend say that made you suddenly decide we should get married?" she asked.

"I've told you before that you needed to have a plan if you were going to have any hope of keeping Hope."

"A plan doesn't mean marriage."

"It's the logical step. Social workers prefer placing babies with couples, rather than single parents."

"But the social workers don't know about Hope."

"That's just the thing. They might."

"What! But how?"

Michael explained what his friend had told him.

"Oh, that's just great," Brett exclaimed, her frantic gaze resting on the baby now asleep once more in her crib. "I'm not going to let them take her away. I'm not!"

"Marry me and they won't be able to take her away."

"You don't know that for sure."

"I know it's your best chance for keeping Hope."

Call her crazy, but Brett found herself actually considering the idea. More than just considering it. She felt as if a powerful voice inside of her was saying "This is your chance at happiness. Go for it!!"

It might not be sensible, not that she'd ever been known for her practicality, but Brett knew that she would accept Michael's surprising proposal. She wasn't going to risk losing Hope. She'd waited so long to get hope back in her life—the baby and the emotion. The possibility of losing all that now made her decision an easy one to make after all. "Okay," she said.

"Good," he replied.

She noticed that he seemed pleased by her acceptance, but not surprised by it. Brett couldn't help wondering if perhaps he'd heard the same voice she had, saying this was his chance at happiness. She immediately dismissed the idea as preposterous. Michael just told her that marriage should be practical. Heaven knows, she'd had first hand knowledge of just how practical some men considered marriage to be.

While Brett had been shuttled around a dozen foster homes during her formative years, throughout it all she'd been raised in a faith that had taught her marriage was first and foremost for procreation. Those beliefs left her feeling totally inadequate after her hysterectomy, as if she'd failed in her role as a woman.

Even now, Michael had only suggested marriage because of the baby, not because of the passionate embrace they'd just shared.

"What happens when we do get married?" she asked him.

"What do you mean what happens?"

"Just that. Do I still live down here or..."

"You and Hope would move in with me. My apartment is a two bedroom. Should the social worker come snooping around, we want to make sure that this looks like a normal marriage."

She winced at his use of the term "normal," feeling it wasn't an adjective that applied to her.

"So Hope and I would sleep in one bedroom and you'd be in the other," she said, wanting to clarify things.

"That's one way of doing it. I'd like to think that eventually you and I would be sharing one bedroom and Hope the other. It's not as if you and I find each other unattractive or anything. Quite the opposite, in fact. When we've kissed it's been..."

"Yes?" she prompted him.

"Inflammable."

She nodded. It was also magical, but she suspected she was the only one who felt this particular brand of magic. Michael felt the chemistry. Sure, that was a starting point, but a part of her couldn't help wishing that he felt more for her. Because she was pretty damn sure she'd fallen hopelessly in love with him.

"So we're agreed, then?" Michael asked. "Getting married is the sensible thing to do. We'll take things one step at a time from there. And once we're married, and things fall into place, we can discreetly go about adopting Hope.''

"It won't be that easy. I know how the system works, remember? When my mom left me, she refused to give up her parental rights, which meant that no one could adopt me. By the time it was legally possible for me to be adopted, I was too old for anyone to want me. When I was about nine, one of my many foster parents finally pointed out the economic realities to me. She told me that chances were I'd never get adopted—foster parents got *paid* for taking care of me as a foster child, but those payments would stop if they adopted me. With a system set up like that, even a nine-year-old could figure out that the odds were stacked against me.''

"So you stopped hoping?"

She was impressed by his astuteness. "That would have been the smart thing to do," she wryly admitted, "but I'm afraid I'm not always awfully smart when it comes to emotions. I'm one of those people who tends to think with their hearts instead of their heads.''

"And I'm the opposite. But maybe that's for the best, you know? Because you need someone with a good head on their shoulders to help balance things out. And I need . . .''

"Yes?" She waited with bated breath to hear what he had to say.

"I need a new shirt," he commented. "Hope has messed this one up but good.''

She tried not to be disappointed by his practical reply. "I'm sorry about that.''

"Don't worry about it. I've got more shirts. Besides, it's something I'd better get used to, huh?'' .

"Are you sure you're ready for this?" Brett asked him quietly. "I've been wanting a baby for some time now. But you . . .''

"I never knew what I was missing. But now that I do, I don't want to miss out on it any longer."

"She'll be teething soon. Keeping you awake nights."

"She's already done that."

"But only a few nights. We're talking weeks here. And think what's ahead, the terrible twos, kindergarten, adolescence, dating, high school...."

"Getting a little ahead of yourself, aren't you?" His voice held a wry humor that made her smile. He had a very sexy voice—deep and rich. It reached out and enfolded her.

"I just want to make sure you know what you're getting into."

"I know. And I know that it won't always be easy. But I also know that it's worth every minute of the effort."

"It's just that people make decisions on the spur of the moment, with all of the best intentions, only to find that they can't cope after all. I saw it happen at foster homes a number of times. A well-meaning family would take you in, not realizing that taking care of someone else's child is different from taking care of your own."

"It shouldn't be," Michael said quietly.

She looked into his eyes and saw no hesitation or wavering there.

"In the end they'd bring me back," Brett whispered.

"It was their loss," he replied, gently caressing her cheek. "I'm not going to take you back like a sweater that doesn't fit, Brett. I've been around, I know what I want. I've never been married before because it never felt right. Now it does. Circumstances might have forced us to move a little faster than we'd like, but the bottom line is that I can see myself being married to you—and I couldn't say that about any other woman I've ever met."

She blinked away the tears. "Then that's good enough for me," she said huskily, pressing his hand to her cheek before letting him go, afraid that he'd feel how much she loved him. Wanting to lessen the tension, she shook a teasing finger at him as she said, "But don't say I didn't warn you."

"I won't. I guess the next step is to get a license and make the other arrangements to get married at city hall. Unless you have an objection to that? Would you prefer a church wedding, at St. Gerald's perhaps?"

"No, city hall would be fine with me."

"Okay, then. That's what we'll do."

"Okay."

"You won't regret it, Brett. I promise you that."

She only wished she could promise him the same thing, that he wouldn't regret it either.


Saturday morning, Michael opened his apartment door only to almost trip over his boots. "What the hel...heck," he muttered, switching words as he caught sight of Consuela Martinez next door. "What are my boots doing out here?"

"I'm sure I have no idea," Consuela replied. "You must have had quite a night last night to have left your boots outside and not even remember doing so."

"It was indeed quite a night," Michael replied. "Brett and I got engaged." Grabbing his boots, he closed his door, satisfied with the older woman's look of startled delight.

Looking down at his boots, he only now realized that they were filled with tangerines and walnuts and brightly wrapped chocolate kisses. A note stuck in one boot said "Better late than never. Happy St. Nicholas's Day!"

Brett! It had to be. Still carrying the boots, he went back out and headed straight for her apartment downstairs, even though he still had no shoes on. The second Brett opened the door, he said, "How did you get your hands on my boots?"

"Good morning to you, too."

He kissed her. It was an exuberant exchange that left her breathless. "What was that for?" she asked.

"You know why. Now tell me, how did you get your hands on my boots? They were next to my bed all night."

"I have no idea what you're talking about," she said demurely.

He waved his boots in her face. "I tell you about St. Nicholas's Day and the next morning I find presents in my boots."

Brett just smiled and shrugged. "It must be magic."

"Yeah, there seems to be a lot of that going around lately."

"There he is," Consuela exclaimed from behind him. "Tell Frieda what you told me," she ordered Michael. "She doesn't believe it. Claims my hearing is going and I misunderstood. Hah! As if there was any misunderstanding what's been going on around here."

"What's she talking about?" Brett asked Michael.

"I told her we were engaged."

"News gets around fast."

"Especially in *this* building," he said. Turning to face Consuela and Frieda, he put his arm around Brett's shoulders and repeated his news. "Congratulate us, we're getting married."

"I told you so," Consuela crowed.

"What are you doing holding your boots like that?" Frieda asked.

"He stumbled over them outside his door this morning," Consuela inserted.

"St. Nicholas visited last night," he said, holding up his boots.

"A little late, wasn't he?" Freida said. "St. Nicholas's Day was three days ago."

"Better late than never," Brett murmured.

* * *

"Hurry up, Brett, or you'll be late for your own wedding!" Keisha exclaimed from outside Brett's bathroom door twelve days later. It may only have taken God six days to create the world, but it took the city of Chicago twelve days to process the paperwork for their marriage.

"There's time yet," Brett replied.

"You wearing that miracle bra I got you for your bridal shower?" Keisha demanded through the closed door. "A bride needs to wear something old, something new, something borrowed, something blue. That bra could be the something new."

Brett eyed her image in the mirror over the sink. Her outfit, which dated back to the thirties, was the something old. It had been a real find at a vintage-clothing thrift shop on Oak Street Keisha had told her about. Brett hadn't been able to resist the funky skirt-and-top combination in ivory lace and silk. The clearance price had been incredibly low, barely twenty dollars. She loved the way the long skirt swirled to midcalf and went well with the whimsical ivory Victorian granny boots she already owned, having gotten a great deal on them the year before. She only owned three other pairs of footwear: her black "interview" pumps, her all-purpose athletic shoes and her sturdy hiking boots—so the fact that the outfit had gone with her Victorian boots had been the deciding factor.

"You fallin' asleep in there, girl?" Keisha impatiently demanded.

"Keep your hat on," Brett replied, adding another coat of lipstick before deciding she looked as good as she could.

Opening the bathroom door, she leaned against the doorjamb and said "Ta-da!"

"Girl, you're looking goooood!" Keisha said, exchanging a high-five hand slap with Brett. "That bra is gonna knock Michael's eyes out."

"Not literally, I hope," Brett murmured, worriedly looking down at her chest as she adjusted a bra strap. "You're sure I look okay? I mean, it doesn't look like I'm wearing padding, does it? Like I'm overdoing it?"

"No way. Now throw those shoulders back and knock 'em dead."

"Thanks for your help today."

"I'm a sucker for romance. I'm just glad you've included me in the preparations. That bridal shower Frieda and Consuela threw for you was a lot more fun than I thought it would be."

"It was so sweet of you all to get me such great things. This bra, the blue garter belt."

"Don't forget the new toolbox."

"As if I would forget. That was really great."

"Okay, we gotta get moving here. You ready to go? What about the something borrowed—you got that hankie from Consuela someplace?"

Brett nodded. "It's stuck in the cleavage of my bra," she said with a grin before giving Keisha a big hug. "Thanks again."

Brett hadn't had much money to spare for this wedding, but with the help of her newfound friends she'd made the most of her allotted budget. Michael had insisted on paying for the license and a pair of simple gold rings.

"You do realize how much diapers cost, right?" she'd asked him again just last night.

"You keep telling me. And yes, I'm still sure about this. So stop worrying."

"A lot of things will change," she'd said.

"I know."

"Scary, isn't it?"

"You, scared? No way," he'd stated with mocking disbelief. "You know, I'm absolutely awed by the way you've fixed things around here."

"Anyone could have done that."

"No, they couldn't. I tried and made a mess of things."

"Consuela told me how you tried working on their bathroom sink without shutting the water off first."

"Their bathroom quickly looked like the middle of Lake Michigan."

Brett smiled at the memory of how she and Michael had laughed together. She hadn't been nervous. In fact, she didn't get nervous until she and Michael and Hope got in the cab that would take them to city hall. Keisha, Frieda and Consuela were in the cab behind them. That's when the jitters set in. Brett tried to keep the panic at bay by concentrating on Hope, who was babbling and pointing out the window.

Noticing Brett's nervousness, Michael said, "Is this bringing back memories of when you were engaged before?"

"Not really. Things were very different then."

Michael took that to mean that she'd been in love with her fiancé then—unlike now, when she was marrying Michael so that she could keep Hope. And that was fine with him. He was better at dealing with practical issues than he was with emotional ones. Brett was the expert in the emotion area. Although he did confess that little Hope had made her way into his heart with the speed of a lightning bolt. And so had Brett.

The thought was in his brain, but he tucked it away in a distant corner, not wanting to deal with it right now.

"Not having any second thoughts, are you?" he asked.

"I confess I'm nervous, but as for having second thoughts...any sane person would, given our situation, but for some reason I'm not. I don't know what that says about me."

"That you have a very good head on your shoulders."

"The ultimate compliment coming from you," she murmured with a laugh. "And not one I've gotten very often in my life."

Brett hadn't gotten enough compliments in her life, if you asked him, but Michael planned on changing that.

At city hall, there were already three other couples ahead of them in the waiting area. Consuela, Frieda and Keisha were taking turns holding Hope, who was delighted with all the attention. After taking off his coat and helping her with hers, Michael sat next to Brett, who was engaged in one of her favorite pastimes—people watching. The youngest couple waiting to get married had their mouths permanently fused together. They were dressed in T-shirts and jeans.

The second couple were dressed in business attire and were complaining about the delay, bemoaning this was messing up their day's schedule. They sat with their datebooks in one hand and flip-phones in the other. "I'm running late with this appointment at city hall," Brett heard the woman saying, "Push back my two o'clock appointment by ten minutes."

Brett might have felt overdressed had it not been for the oldest couple. The man appeared to be well known to the staff. "You back here again, Ray?" one of the women behind the counter greeted him.

Ray wore a red-and-green crocheted vest over his red shirt. His hat had Ho-Ho-Ho written on the side of it. His bride-to-be looked like she'd been a Vegas showgirl at one time—in the fifties, maybe. She wore green. Lots of it. With satin ruffles decorated with spangles all around her bare and rather bony shoulders.

"What is this, your eighth marriage, Ray?" the city-hall worker asked.

"Only my seventh," Ray replied.

"Gypsies believe that seven is a lucky number," Michael whispered in her ear.

Brett tried to hide her grin but couldn't.

"That's better," he said approvingly. "You were starting to look as green as Hope's spinach baby food, or that woman's awful dress."

"You say the sweetest things, you silver-tongued devil," she retorted, her voice laced with mockery.

"You look lovely."

"Yeah, right. Green and lovely."

"Hey, it works for Kermit the Frog."

"You've been reading Hope's books again."

"She loves it when I read to her," Michael said.

Brett knew why. The baby loved hearing his voice. So did Brett. She could listen to him forever. He made Kermit and Miss Piggy sound like Shakespeare. She was willing to bet that even if Michael were to read one of those stupid tags that came on new pillows—he'd still sound wonderfully sexy. Or reading the instructions for filling out a tax form. Anything. It was his voice. It was magic.

She nervously clutched his hand.

"Yes, I know how much diapers cost," he reassured her with a grin.

"You're just a sucker for a woman in distress," she countered.

"No, I'm a sucker for a woman who knows her way around a toolbox and a baby with equal skill."

"Not yet. I'm still more experienced with the toolbox."

"You do great with Hope. You got all those baby books out of the library and read them all."

"There's a lot I don't know yet."

"So we'll learn together."

*We* and *together.* Two of the best words in the English language, she decided.

"You think Hope is going to sleep through the ceremony?" she asked, noticing the way the baby's head was bobbing against Consuela's shoulder.

"Knowing how the kid likes chaos, probably," Michael replied. "If the judge is loud enough."

The judge was loud enough and Hope did indeed sleep through the entire ceremony, which was brief and over before Brett knew what had happened.

"You may now kiss the bride," the judge said impatiently, clearly in a hurry to get on to the next couple on his appointment schedule.

The strange thing was, Brett didn't *feel* married. Not even when Michael kissed her. She felt warm and tingly all over, as she did whenever he kissed her. But married? That should feel different, no?

She was hugged by Keisha and Frieda before they were all rushed out of the room. Two cabs whisked them back to Love Street, where a huge sign that said Just Married hung on the door to Michael's apartment. It seems that while they were at city hall, Mr. and Mrs. Stephanopolis had been busy decorating the place. White and pink crepe paper hung from every inch of the door frame, blocking their entrance.

"Are you sure you don't want us to keep Hope overnight?" Consuela asked hopefully.

"No, thanks for the offer."

"Well, then we'll just keep her for two hours more so you and Michael can enjoy the bridal dinner Mrs. Stephanopolis made for you both."

"The dinner is all ready to be served," Mrs. Stephanopolis said. "The main course is in the covered chafing dishes. Just go on in and enjoy."

With those words, everyone rushed off to their own place, Consuela and Frieda cooing over Hope as they left Brett and Michael alone.

"Mrs. Stephanopolis must have snitched the key to your place from my building key ring when I was working at her apartment," Brett said uncertainly, unable to judge from Michael's expression how he felt about all this hoopla. "Sorry about all the fuss." She reached out to undo the tape holding the crepe-paper barrier in place.

"I like it," Michael surprised her by saying. Then he surprised her even further by sweeping her up in his arms.

"What are you doing?" she gulped, wishing she hadn't eaten so much food at the bridal shower the night before.

"Why, you're just a little thing!" he noted in wonder.

Giving him a dark frown, she stuck out her chest. "Watch who you're calling little," she growled.

"I am watching," he said with a devilish grin as he made the most of his unrestricted view of the shadowy valley between her breasts. "And enjoying every moment."

She felt the heat warming her cheeks as she blushed.

"Hold on," he said as he leaned over to open the door before easily bursting through the paper swags across the doorway. "Welcome to your new home, Mrs. Janos," he murmured, in no hurry as he slowly let her slide against his body before finally setting her on her feet.

"Wonderful," she said dreamily, basking in the unadulterated elation washing over her. The intimate contact she'd just shared with him had generated a feeling of... Words simply failed her. How did you describe this secret joy? She couldn't. All she could do was hug the feeling inside, keeping it deep in her heart.

Entranced by her glowing face, Michael didn't even hear what she'd said. "What?"

Seeing his quizzical look, she strove to gather her dazzled senses. "I mean the *table* looks wonderful. Mr. and Mrs. Stephanopolis have really outdone themselves, don't you think?"

He nodded, moving closer to the table, and pulled out a chair for her.

"Thank you," she murmured as she sat down, feeling shy and awkward.

Wine was chilling and the candles were already lit. Someone had set the Rom box in the middle of the table as a centerpiece. The box appeared to glow in the candle-light.

"I got my copy of the signed prenuptial agreement in the mail this morning," Michael said, his matter-of-fact tone contrasting with the romantic surroundings.

Taking her cue from him, Brett replied, "I got mine to-day, too. Having a prenup seemed the sensible thing to do." Actually, she'd suggested it for Michael's protection. She didn't want him worrying that she'd fleece him or anything. "Since a friend of mine from Loyola is now an attorney, she did it as a favor for me."

"So you said. What about your classes at Loyola? We never discussed whether or not you plan on continuing them, now that Hope is here."

"I haven't exactly been on the fast track to success," she wryly pointed out. "I've been taking courses as time and money allow. I don't anticipate that changing. I'll have plenty of time to take care of Hope. I'm only registered for one class next semester."

Michael almost said "I know" before remembering that he wasn't supposed to have that information, that he'd gotten it through the background check he'd run on her. Brett hadn't mentioned it before. Afraid he might trip up again, he said, "Uh, I guess we should start eating, huh?"

She nodded and picked up her fork.

They had a tender Greek salad for starters. Brett knew there were black olives in the salad, but was later unable to remember what else she ate. It all tasted delicious, but she was too distracted to focus on food. No, her thoughts were consumed with satisfying another kind of appetite.

She stole a discreet look at his mouth. The angular line of his jaw was starting to show the shadow of a day's growth of beard. Knowing she'd be lost if she got caught up in the magic of his awesome eyes, she kept her gaze lowered for most of the meal. The peek she'd gotten of his lips had already stirred her up enough as it was. Grabbing her fork, she attacked the piece of wedding cake on her dessert plate with unladylike gusto.

The knock on the door made her jump a foot. "Calm down," he murmured, pausing on his way to answer the door to place a reassuring hand on her shoulder for a moment before moving on.

"Oh, you two are still eating," Frieda said.

"I told you we should keep the baby longer," Consuela maintained from her side.

"No, that's okay," Brett said, hurrying to the door. "We were just about done anyway."

"Here, I'll take Hope," Michael said, smoothly transferring the little girl to the crook of his arm. "She'll get your lovely dress dirty," he reminded Brett.

"I'll go change." She almost headed out the door to her place downstairs before remembering she lived with Michael now and most of her clothes were still boxed in a corner of the second bedroom she would be sharing with Hope.

Meanwhile Consuela was saying, "Are you sure we took enough pictures at city hall? Maybe we should snap some more while they're still dressed up."

"You used up three rolls of film already," Frieda retorted.

"I guess you're right. It's just that everyone looks so nice."

"Thanks again for lending us so many baby things," Brett told Consuela, smoothing the lacy white dress that Hope was wearing.

Everyone laughed as Hope chose that moment to abruptly tug down the elastic lacy band in her hair so that it rested smack across the bridge of her nose. She looked so adorably confused. Brett knew the feeling.

Seeing the devoted look on Michael's face, she reminded herself that it was as clear as the hair band Hope wore on her cute little nose that he adored the baby. Brett had done the right thing marrying him. But it wasn't right that she should get greedy, wanting more from him than he was able to give . . . wanting his love.

Later, as she watched him getting the baby ready for bed, wiggling Hope's toes while reciting This Little Pig Went to the Play-offs, she stomped out wishful thoughts and firmly reminded herself that he'd only married her for the baby. Same reason she'd married him. The fact that she loved him should play no part in their relationship. Not until he felt the same way. If he ever did.

Putting his arm around Brett, Michael stood next to her as they watched Hope settle down to sleep in her crib. Feeling how stiffly Brett held herself, he misunderstood her reasons. "You can relax," he reassured her. "I'm not going to be sweeping you off your feet again tonight. We've got plenty of time to get used to this marriage stuff. There's no rush, right?"

"Right." To him it was marriage stuff. To her it was the secret longing of a heart that had almost forgotten how to hope.


"Where do you want me to put this box?" Michael asked the next day.

"Just put it in the living room for now," she answered from the kitchen, where she was child-proofing the lower cabinet doors so they couldn't be opened by Hope's curious little fingers. Brett had already put in the electric outlet guards and installed a protective grate in front of all the radiators.

"The living room? I can hardly get in there as it is," he muttered, surveying the room already filled with boxes of baby things.

"I couldn't hear you. What did you say?"

"Nothing." Michael set the box on top of the others already placed against one wall. They'd moved most of her furniture earlier in the day, not that she had much of it. She'd offered to have the gang from the youth center help again, but Michael had firmly maintained that he could do it on his own.

He was just about to take a breather and sit down in his recliner when there was a knock at the door. "I'll get it," he shouted.

Opening the door, he found his parents and his sister standing on the other side.

"Sorry for dropping by unannounced," Gaylynn said, "but Mom and Dad wanted to stop by on their way home from the airport."

"I couldn't wait any longer," his mom said, as she put her arms around his shoulders and hugged him. "We've been gone so long!"

Seeing the packed boxes and general mayhem in the living room, his father said, "What's going on here? You moving again already?"

"No, Dad, I'm not moving. I just got married."

# Seven

Michael's sister Gaylynn was the first to break the stunned silence. "You're kidding, right?" she said.

"No, I'm not kidding." Seeing Brett standing on the kitchen threshold, he took her by the arm and brought her over. "This is Brett, my wife."

"You really *are* married?" Gaylynn asked, voicing the astonishment reflected on his parents' faces.

"I just said I was, didn't I?" he replied irritably.

"Nice going, Michael. Why don't you just hit them over the head with a hammer?" Brett said in exasperation.

"She's a handyman," he explained to his family. "She's great with things like hammers."

"She's a *man?*" his mother repeated in confused horror.

Knowing how his mother avidly watched the tabloid talk shows, he hastened to reassure her. "Calm down, Mom. You're not going to be seeing us on an episode of Oprah, or anything like that. I just meant that I hired Brett to be the building supervisor, to fix things up. That's how we first met.''

"And when was this?" his mother demanded.

"Almost a month ago."

"This marriage was rather sudden, then."

"It's the box," his father suddenly said. "It is responsible."

Michael sighed. "Now, Dad, don't start with the omens."

"If your right ear tingles, that is an omen. The box is *bahtali*.''

"What are you two talking about?" his mother demanded.

"His great-aunt Magda sent him a box," his dad answered.

"Our son just got married and you have nothing better to do than talk about boxes?"

"It's a Rom box," his dad explained.

Pointing at Brett, his mother said, "And she's an American wife. How do you do," Mrs. Janos continued with old-world charm. "Your name is Brett, that is right?"

Brett nodded.

"Well, Brett, I would like to be the first to welcome you to our crazy family."

Brett swallowed the nervous lump in her throat. Or tried to. It took her two attempts before she could say anything. "Thank you, Mrs. Janos."

"You must call me Maria. And this is my husband, Konrad. And my daughter, Gaylynn."

"Is that a baby I hear crying?" Gaylynn asked.

"It's Hope," Brett replied. "She's crying because she woke up and Michael wasn't there."

"The baby is yours?" Maria asked.

"The baby is *ours*," Michael said.

His mother looked ready to faint.

"We're going to be adopting her," Brett quickly explained. "The baby isn't actually biologically ours."

"I think I need to sit down," his mother said. She took a few more steps into the apartment.

"I'm sorry the place is kind of a mess," Brett apologized, grabbing a baby blanket from one of the lawn chairs that provided additional seating in the living room. "I just moved my things in yesterday and today and we haven't finishing unpacking yet. It might be better if we sat in the kitchen. That room's tidier."

"Because we never go in there," Michael said before Brett elbowed him in the ribs.

"I'll just go get Hope," Brett said, making her escape.

In the relative safety of the baby's room, she picked up Hope and cuddled her soothingly, her mind jumbled with impressions of her new in-laws. Michael's dad had the same high cheekbones and intense eyes as his son. His mother exuded old-world class. His sister, with her shoulder-length light brown hair and brown eyes, seemed direct and friendly—someone Brett could relate to. But would Gaylynn, or any of his family, relate to *her*? That was the question.

"Miklos, you had best explain from the beginning," Michael's mother said in that no-nonsense voice she only used when he'd done something outrageous, like climbing on top of the roof when he was seven. Actually, she hadn't used his given name once since then.

"It's kind of a long story...." he began.

"We're not going anyplace. I will make tea while you talk and try to explain why you could not wait a few days to have your own parents at your wedding." Maria marched into the kitchen, expecting her family to follow.

They did.

"It wasn't a church wedding or anything like that. We went down to city hall," Michael said as he sat at the table with his father and sister.

"You didn't marry on the 14th, did you? That's a bad day for marriage," his father stated.

"No, it wasn't on the 14th. It was the 21st," Michael replied.

His mother was not pleased. "Yesterday? You got married yesterday? You couldn't wait one more day for us to come home? Why the hurry?"

"Because of the baby. We want to adopt her as soon as possible."

"And that's another thing." She waved a teaspoon at him. "Since when have you gotten along with babies?"

"Since Hope. Wait 'til you see her, Mom. Then you'll know what I mean. She's special. A real heartbreaker."

"You have never noticed babies before."

"That's because they always screamed whenever I got near them."

"It sounded as if this baby has a good set of lungs as well," his mother noted.

"Yeah, she does," Michael ruefully acknowledged. "But she stops crying when I hold her."

"This I have to see to believe," his sister said.

"She wants you, Michael," Brett said as she brought the fussing baby into the kitchen.

Michael held his arms out for the little girl, astonishing his family with the ease with which he held the baby—who indeed stopped crying as soon as she was in his arms.

"You certainly do look like a pro," Gaylynn noted admiringly.

"I've had plenty of practice over the past couple of weeks," Michael admitted with a laugh.

"I am still waiting for an explanation," his mother reminded him, her frosty demeanor melting as Hope gave her a drooling grin over Michael's shoulder. "Oh, she is adorable! Will she let me hold her?"

"Sure she will," Michael replied. "Won't you, Hope? You ready to meet your new grandparents, kiddo?"

While his mom held Hope and the rest of his family cooed and fussed over the baby, Michael used the opportunity to take Brett aside and have a private word with her. "I know I told you that it would be safe going to the police, and that sort of blew up in our faces, but I'd like to tell my family the truth," he said quietly. "They won't betray our confidence. They won't tell anyone if we ask them not to. What do you say?"

Brett knew that, given the hurried manner in which she and Michael had gotten married, his family was bound to have questions. "We have to tell them something and the truth would probably be the best thing. You've certainly botched things up so far," she added irritably.

"I wasn't expecting them to drop by so soon."

"Yeah, well, this time let me do the explaining," she said.

In the end, Brett simply told his family the truth, from her finding Hope in the foyer to the social worker hot on their trail.

Brett ended by saying, "I lived in foster homes for most of my childhood. I just couldn't bear the thought of Hope ending up in that system." She briefly considered telling them about the hysterectomy she'd had, but couldn't seem to screw up the courage. Her confidence was precarious enough as it was and facing his family unexpectedly this way had used up what courage she had for the time being.

"We needed to move fast or risk losing Hope," Michael stated.

"One must never lose hope," his mother said with a sweet smile.

"Thanks, Mom. I knew you'd understand."

Hugs were exchanged all around as Hope gurgled with quiet pleasure.

Later, as Brett and his mother and sister fussed over the baby, Michael took his father aside in the living room to talk about the box.

"So come on, Dad. I've been waiting for weeks now. What's the deal with the box?"

"It holds a Rom love charm that has hit every second generation of Janoses since...the early 18th century, I think."

"A love charm?" Michael repeated in disbelief.

His father nodded.

"That only hits every second generation?"

"That's right."

"And who would that be?"

"You, Gaylynn and Dylan, of course."

"Great."

"Do you want to hear the legend or not?" his father retorted.

"Sorry. Go ahead."

"Family legend has it that a beautiful young Rom girl fell in love with a nobleman but their love was forbidden, because he was a count...."

"A no-account, if you ask me," Gaylynn inserted as she joined them.

"No one did ask you," Michael retorted.

"If this is a family legend, I have as much right to hear it as you." Noticing Michael's glance toward the kitchen, Gaylynn said, "Brett and Mom are getting along like long-lost pals. They'll talk for ages yet. Go on with the story, Papa." That was what she called their father.

"Where was I?" Konrad asked.

"At the part where the beautiful Gypsy girl fell for a no-account count," Gaylynn replied.

"Ah, yes. The count did not return her feelings, so the girl paid to have a love spell cast on her behalf. To pay for it, she brought with her the only thing of value she had, an engraved box that had been in her family for generations. The problem was that the spell was done by a *shuvani* who got things messed up. Regretting her error, she let the girl keep the box and would accept nothing for the spell."

"What do you mean exactly by messed up?" Gaylynn asked.

"The spell skipped a generation—every second generation of Janos children would find love 'Where they looked for it'—which was taken literally! The first person of the opposite sex that they saw after opening the charmed box was the person they would fall in love with and vice versa. We are direct descendants of that original Rom girl."

"How come I never heard this family story before?" Michael asked.

"It is no mere *story*," his father replied. "The charmed box is real and is said to have caused some unusual relationships in the past. I said nothing before because the spell did not apply to your mother and myself. But your grandparents..." His father shook his head. "It hit them hard, this love charm. My mother was a talented violinist. She even played with the Budapest Philharmonic Orchestra in the 1930s. She'd gotten the box when her grandmother died. My father was a much younger car mechanic who was fixing her car at the time. One look and they were in love. Then World War II broke out and my father was drafted. During the war, my mother was nearly sent to a concentration camp because of her Rom blood. As it was, she was devastated when my father was killed on the last day of the war. I was their only child. She lived long enough to see me married, but it has been my lifelong sorrow that she died before any of you children were born...." His father blinked away the tears. "She would have been proud to have such good grandchildren."

Gaylynn hugged their father while Michael squeezed his shoulder in a form of silent communication. Konrad Janos was a man of deep emotion, be it pain or joy. He displayed both with equal zest. It didn't matter if the emotion had first occurred decades or days ago—the intensity remained.

Taking a deep breath, Konrad continued, "Your great-aunt Magda was your grandmother's sister. She's the one who sent the box to you, Michael. I remember Magda swearing that she'd never open the box when it came to her as the next in line after your grandmother's death. It goes to siblings first, oldest to youngest and then remains there until it is time for the second generation. As far as I know, Magda never did open the box and she certainly never married. Who did you look at when you first opened it, son?"

Michael's eyes shift to Brett, in the kitchen.

"Ah, so it was Brett you first saw. Then this marriage between you two is a love match, after all," his father said with a twinkle in his eyes. "And with you living on *Love* Street, it is indeed *bahtali.*"

Michael shook his head. "I told you, we married for the baby."

His father waved away the words. "It was the charmed box working."

"What about the key inside the box? What does the legend have to say about that?" Michael asked him.

Konrad shook his head. "I know nothing about a key. Show it to me."

Michael went to get the box, which had been sitting on his stereo. But it wasn't there any longer. "Brett," he called out. "Do you know where the Rom box is?"

"No," she called back from the kitchen. "It might have gotten misplaced what with all the mayhem of my moving in and trying to child-proof your apartment."

"That's okay," Konrad reassured Michael. "You can show me the box next time. On Christmas Eve, perhaps? You are coming over along with Brett and Hope, no?"

"You bet."

"I'm sorry I don't know anything about the contents of the box," Konrad said. "I do know that there were other stories of couples affected by this love-charmed box in earlier times. I can't recall them at the moment, but I know your mother wrote the stories down as my mother told them to us when we were still in the old country. They are with the family papers."

"I just thought you might know what the key is supposed to open. Maybe a room in an old house, because the key is a very old type not commonly used these days. It looks like it's sterling silver and is intricately engraved."

"Did you ever consider that this mysterious key might be to your heart?" his father wryly suggested.

"Come on, Dad. You know I don't believe in magic."

"Magic is just making something happen that you want to happen. There is no fighting it. The Old Ways are powerful and are not to be trifled with. Remember that and all will be well."

"Do you think Hope is too young to understand what's going on?" Brett asked Michael as she pushed the baby's stroller through the crowds at Chicago's Museum of Science and Industry.

"She's old enough to have a good time," he replied before demanding, "What have you got in this diaper bag? It weighs a ton."

"Going out with a baby requires a lot of stuff…bottles, blanket, diapers, diaper-rash ointment, toys."

"Twenty-pound weights," he added to the list.

"Oh darn, I left the weights at home," she returned with a grin.

"You look as excited as Hope is."

"I've always loved coming to see the Christmas Around the World exhibit. I remember the first time I visited it…I must have been about four. I was staying with a nice family—she always smelled like vanilla. And they brought me here to see the trees. They looked huge to me. I'd never seen so many ornaments. I've never forgotten it. They moved me from that foster home shortly after the holidays. I'm not sure why, I think maybe she was going to have a baby. Anyway, I wasn't able to make it back to the museum until I was thirteen, when I came on my own. As I walked past the tree from Sweden, I decided I'd visit there someday. I went around the entire exhibit and picked which countries to visit based entirely by the way they decorated their trees. Of course, it was just a dream. I've never done any traveling. Not yet, anyway. But someday maybe..."

To her surprise, Michael said, "It's good to have dreams."

"I'll bet last month you never dreamed you'd be a married man, pushing a baby stroller."

"I'm not the one pushing the stroller, you are."

As they neared the entrance to the exhibit, she said, "I don't think Hope is going to be able to see from her stroller. Maybe you should pick her up. You can set the baby bag in the stroller then."

"Good idea. Hope weighs less than this bag does, don't you, stinky britches?"

Brett rolled her eyes at his latest nickname for the baby, a result of her having him change Hope's diapers.

Walking behind them, Brett got the biggest kick out of watching the way Hope's eyes widened and blinked in awe at the trees Michael was so meticulously pointing out to her. She hid a smile when Michael read the signs aloud to Hope. The baby babbled along with him. He didn't even seem to notice that Hope was drooling all over his nice shirt. But Brett did, and she reached into the baby bag for a cloth to wipe the baby's mouth. When Brett straightened, she found a beautiful woman talking to Michael.

"Mike! What a surprise to find you here! I thought you hated crowds. Oh, my God, I don't believe it! You're holding a baby!"

"What's so strange about that?" he said defensively.

"Come on. You with a baby? You've got to admit it makes a wild picture. The man who gets nervous if a woman even comments about his furniture or lack thereof?"

"I've changed."

"In a month? I saw you at the beginning of November. We went to that little French place for dinner, remember?" Her voice dropped seductively as she laid her hand on his arm.

"I'm married now," Michael announced in a loud voice.

"Get out of town!" The woman playfully drew her finger down his chest. "Is this some kind of joke?"

"Do you see me laughing?" he retorted curtly, stepping away from her touch.

The woman stared at him in surprise. "But you said there was no way you'd tie yourself down with the chains of matrimony. Why, just a few weeks ago, you were bragging that the woman hadn't been born who could make you give up your independence."

"I changed my mind," he muttered.

Raising an eyebrow at her new husband, Brett said, "Aren't you going to introduce me to your little friend, Michael?"

Brett hoped she didn't sound as jealous as she felt. The woman was gorgeous, not a hair out of place, her nails done to perfection. Her outfit was perfectly accessorized.

And then there was Brett—in her trademark black leggings and the blue sweater that was almost as old as she was. Her nails had no polish, and working on replacing Consuela and Freida's shower head the day before had resulted in her ripping the only decent-looking nail she'd had left. She'd forgotten to put on lipstick when they'd left the apartment this morning, a perennial shortcoming of hers. One of many. Her only jewelry was her wedding ring and a no-nonsense watch. Oh, and a pair of silver Christmas-tree earrings in her ears. Hardly the picture of sophistication.

"Brett, this is . . ."

"Adrienne," the perfect woman said with a smile that could have graced any toothpaste ad. "And you are?"

"Michael's wife." Brett deliberately made a show out of using her left hand, with its wedding band, to brush her bangs away from her eyes. Next to flashing the ring under Adrienne's nose, it was as close as she could get to flaunting the fact that she was married.

"And when was the happy event, Mike?" Adrienne asked. "None of your friends seem to know about it."

"We had a private ceremony," Michael said.

Adrienne raised her brows, then gave Brett the once-over before nodding her head understandingly as if to say *Yes, I can see why you wouldn't want any of your friends knowing you'd married this shoddy-looking woman.* Aloud she merely said, "I can't believe you're married."

"Believe it," Brett replied in a no-nonsense voice.

Michael put his free arm around her as if to restrain her from punching Adrienne's lights out. "We're holding up the line. We'd better be moving on."

Moving on? He'd probably done that a lot with the women in his past, Brett thought sourly.

"I'll give you a call after the holidays and we'll get together. With the rest of your friends. A party. You can come, too, if you'd like, Bitsy," Adrienne said in a patronizing voice.

Brett's temper flared at the other woman's blatant rudeness. "The name is Brett, lady, and what I'd like to do is . . ."

"Move on," Michael hurriedly inserted. "That's what we'd like to do. See you." Taking Brett by the arm, he moved around the corner to the next row of trees.

"We're changing our phone number," Brett declared the moment Adrienne was gone.

"I only dated the woman once."

"Is that all you did with her? Date her?"

"Yes."

"You two were never . . . you know." Brett wiggled her hand.

"No, we were never . . . you know," he said, teasingly repeating her words and hand gesture.

Two trees down the row, Brett spoke again. "She called you Mike."

"A two-syllable name is too long for Adrienne to manage," he stated dryly.

Brett grinned and smacked his arm. Hope, thinking they were playing a game, chortled in delight and smacked him in the jaw in the process.

"Ow! The two women in my life are ganging up on me," Michael grumbled.

His comment didn't distract Brett from the matter at hand. "If you had such a low opinion of Adrienne, then why did you ask her out?"

"I didn't. She asked me."

"Then why did you say yes?"

"I was dumber then."

"Dumber, huh?"

He nodded.

"I suppose that's as good an excuse as any," she allowed.

As a rowdy bunch of teenagers pushed by, Michael protectively drew Brett closer, his arm shielding her from the rest of the world. "I have better taste now," he whispered in Brett's ear, leaving her wishing he'd nibble her earlobe while he was there.

"Not everyone would agree with you on that," she breathlessly replied.

"More fools they," he murmured before releasing her.

As the family gathered together around Michael's parents' Christmas tree, Brett lifted her glass for a toast.

"*Egészégére!*" Konrad said, clinking his shot glass with those held by the rest of the family.

Brett couldn't even attempt to repeat that toast so she gave one of her own. "*Salut!*"

Copying their actions, she drank the shot glass full of clear, cold liquid in one gulp.

"It's not as good as *házi pálinka*...homemade *pálinka,*" Konrad partially translated. "But this will do."

"Whaaa...whaaat is this?" Brett gasped when she finally got her voice back.

"Pear brandy," Michael replied, rubbing his hand on her back. "You okay?"

"Sure," she said, wondering why her voice sounded like Lauren Bacall's all of a sudden. "I didn't need those vocal cords anyway."

"I guess *pálinka* can be a little overpowering at first," Michael acknowledged.

"Dylan claims our entire family is a little overpowering at first," Gaylynn noted with a grin.

"Dylan is my younger brother," Michael explained for Brett's benefit. "He's the rolling stone in the family."

"He called earlier today," Maria said. "He's in New Mexico, I think he said."

"I got a card from him two weeks ago," Michael stated.

"Did you get a Christmas card from your friend Hunter Davis down in North Carolina?" Gaylynn casually asked her brother.

"Yeah, I did. He's easier to keep track of than Dylan. That postcard I got from our baby brother was from Oklahoma, not New Mexico."

"I don't think that boy will ever settle down," Maria said with a shake of her head.

"And I don't think we're going to have time to open our presents before dinner if we don't hurry up and get started," Gaylynn pointed out.

"Oh, you," her mother said with a laughing wave of her hand. "You were always the impatient one. You were even born three weeks early."

"Now, Mama, Brett doesn't want to hear about my baby stories. Right, Brett?"

Brett just shrugged her shoulders and rubbed her throat.

"Good time to lose your voice," Michael said approvingly. "Don't let my sister get you into trouble."

"I can get into trouble all by myself," Brett couldn't resist retorting.

"Time to open presents," Konrad declared with a clap of his hands. After saying a short prayer, he reached down under the tree for a gaily wrapped present. "Here's one for you, Brett."

Brett had never opened presents so early before. It wasn't even dark yet, but Michael had explained that dinner began as soon as the first star gleamed in the sky and presents were always opened before Christmas dinner at his parents' house.

Hope was sitting in her bounce chair, squealing with excitement as wrapping paper flew in all directions. Seconds later Brett sat speechless at the beautifully embroidered red vest in her lap.

"Do you like it?" Maria asked.

Brett nodded.

"Good."

"Red brings good luck," Konrad told her. "Open this one next," he added, handing her a smaller package.

Inside this one was a tiny vest for Hope, also in red. "It's a mother-daughter set," Maria explained. "I made them before Gaylynn's birth. Now I want you and Hope to have them.''

"I don't know what to say," Brett whispered.

Maria patted her on the shoulder understandingly. "Let's see if it fits Hope, shall we?"

Of course the little vest looked adorable on her.

"Wait, there's a present I got myself that I need to open before we begin," Michael said, opening a square box under the tree. It was a video camera, already loaded with tape and ready to go. Of course, he'd tried it out ahead of time, not wanting to look like a dummy, so now he was able to catch the festivities on tape.

Then everyone started opening presents in rotation so that each could ooh and aah over the goodies received. Brett had bought Michael the one thing he'd told her he needed—a new shirt. She'd gotten him something else, but had chickened out on giving him the black silk boxer shorts at the last minute. Ten minutes later she was stunned to see them in a box he'd just opened.

"Where did those come from?" she asked in a croaky voice.

"The ticket says they're from you."

For a brief second the option of denying any knowledge flashed through her mind. Indeed, she had no idea how they'd gotten under the tree. Granted, she'd rushed around in a hurry wrapping stuff this morning, but she could have sworn she'd left those wickedly rich shorts in the bag to be returned. She'd seen them in that specialty lingerie shop Keisha's sister worked at, and had immediately pictured Michael wearing them.

"*Are* they from you?" Michael asked.

"Yeah," she said, her chin lifting defensively.

"Thanks," he murmured, his eyes alight with a naughty gleam that would have done any Gypsy pirate proud. "You ready to open my present for you now?"

Not trusting herself to speak, since her tongue felt as if it would trip over itself if she did, she merely nodded before taking the small box he handed her.

"It's small to be a hammer," she noted teasingly.

"I wouldn't say that," he replied as she opened the velvet box to find a tiny gold hammer hanging from a serpentine chain. "Do you like it?" he prompted when she just stared at it.

"It's beautiful," she whispered. "Thank you." She gave him a quick hug, not wanting to embarrass him by showing too much affection in front of his family.

"The first star is almost out," Konrad declared. "We'd better finish up here so we can start dinner."

Michael took a final shot of Hope with her head covered with bows from the presents they'd unwrapped before the entire family sat down to an abundant although meatless meal. They had cabbage soup to start, followed by fish, noodles, fresh vegetables and twisted Christmas bread. For dessert they had cakes shaped like horseshoes—for good luck—and filled with poppy seeds.

"The two mainstays of Hungarian cooking are paprika and poppy seeds," Michael was kiddingly saying.

"Hungarian paprika is good for you," his mother retorted. "It has lots of vitamin C."

"Vitamin C having, in fact, been discovered by a Hungarian scientist," Gaylynn inserted.

"You can tell my sister's a teacher," Michael said. "Always showing off her superior brain."

Gaylynn responded by tossing her napkin at him.

"Children!" Maria clucked her tongue disapprovingly. "Behave at the table. Little Hope has better manners."

"You haven't seen her with a jar of strained carrots," Michael said. "It's not a pretty picture."

"I should get out the picture of you as a baby. The one with your entire face and hair smeared full of butter."

Michael frowned. "No, you shouldn't get that picture out, Mom. I think I burned it last time you got it out."

"Not the negative," Gaylynn retorted.

"She's got one of you naked on the rug," Michael reminded his sister.

Watching the good-natured squabbling, Brett delighted in the feeling of being part of a family. With Hope in a high chair beside her, and Michael seated on her other side, Brett felt truly blessed. Even though it wasn't white, the earlier snow having melted and no more having fallen, this was the best Christmas she'd ever had.

And it wasn't over yet. After dinner, they all sang carols while Maria played the piano. Michael had a beautiful voice, as did his father, although they both laughed about how Dylan couldn't hold a tune to save his life.

"The priest even asked him not to sing while in church, but to just mouth the words," Konrad recalled as they prepared to head for midnight services.

Brett was talking to Maria when Gaylynn took Michael aside and said, "Here I thought I was the fearless one in the family, yet you're the one who jumps right into marriage. But having met Brett, I can see why. I like her, big brother. You did good for once."

"I'm so glad you approve," he retorted mockingly.

"I thought you would be," Gaylynn shot back with a grin. "Merry Christmas," she added before giving him a hug.

He gave her one of his trademark bear hugs in return. "Merry Christmas, kiddo."

It was only when Michael got back to his own place that he remembered that he never had gotten around to finding the Rom box and his dad never had gotten around to telling him more stories about it.

Brett restlessly tossed in bed, wanting to wake up but unable to. She was having a nightmare, and try as she could, she couldn't escape its slumberous clutches. In her dream she and Michael and Hope were gathered under a Christmas tree, celebrating the holidays. Everything had been perfect. Then someone walked into the room and took the baby from her arms.

"That's not your baby," the woman had screamed at Brett. "She's mine! Not yours. Mine! *Not* yours. *Mine!*"

The words kept repeating themselves.

Brett tried to call out, tried to reach out to Hope...tried to move...but she was frozen in place, a scream lodged in her throat.

"N-n-n-o-o-o-o!!!"

The sound of her own voice finally woke Brett.

A second later, Michael burst into her room, wearing nothing but the black silk boxer shorts Brett had given him for Christmas.

# Eight

Sitting beside her on the bed, Michael whispered her name as he took her in his arms. Brett rested her face against his bare shoulder, her heart racing with fear from the aftermath of the vivid nightmare as she gasped for breath.

"Shh, love. It'll be okay," he murmured reassuringly, threading his fingers through her hair. "It was just a dream."

"But it seemed so real," she whispered.

"What did, love? What were you dreaming that was so bad?"

"She took Hope away."

"Who did?" he asked, rubbed his thumb across her nape. With every gentle stroke he comforted and aroused her at the same time.

"I don't know. Some woman. We were sitting next to the Christmas tree and I was so happy. She said Hope was hers. I didn't recognize her but she took Hope from my arms. She took her *away!*"

"Shh. Hope is right in her crib. Look." He leaned away so Brett could get a clear line of vision to the sleeping baby.

Seeing her, Brett felt both relieved and silly for having overreacted to what was, after all, just a bad dream. She'd had them before while growing up. Plenty of them. So many, in fact, that she'd frequently been reprimanded. *Don't be a nuisance, Brett.* The words echoed in her head.

Here she was doing it again, being a nuisance—waking Michael in the middle of the night and almost waking the baby as well.

She pulled away from his embrace. Lifting her hand to her face, she found it still damp from the tears she'd shed while sleeping. "I'm sorry." Self-consciously, she wiped her cheeks with her trembling fingers. "I didn't mean to wake you up. Go back to bed. I'll be fine now. *Please,* go back to bed."

Michael had no intention of leaving her. "Scoot over," he said.

She automatically did so, before thinking to question his actions. "What are you doing?"

Lifting the covers, he joined her in the twin bed, pulling the bedclothes back around them. Gently easing her into his embrace, he matter-of-factly settled her against him, spoon-fashion. "Go back to sleep," he whispered against her ear. "I'll be right here."

"I can't sleep with you here."

"Sure you can." He shifted his arm so that it rested around her waist, making sure to keep his hand away from her breasts. And then he started telling her about the Christmases he and his family had shared over the years. He was deliberately using a soothing monotone intended to put her at ease and put her back to sleep.

Only when he felt her relax and heard the even breathing that told him she was asleep, only then did he lightly kiss the vulnerable pale skin at her nape. "You're not alone anymore," he told her. "And you never will be again."

"I never heard of Boxing Day before, but now that I have, I think I could get used to the idea," Keisha was telling Brett the day after Christmas as the two women stood near the buffet table laden with food.

"I read about Boxing Day when I was a kid visiting the Christmas Around the World exhibit at the museum," Brett said as she nibbled on a *pfeffernüsse* cookie Frieda had brought.

"They still do that? I went there on a field trip from grade school one time."

"Yeah, they still do that. Michael, Hope and I went last week. Anyway, once I was on my own I started having a Boxing Day party the day after Christmas. It's a great way to share leftovers."

"You got that right," Keisha agreed, sampling more of Consuela's salsa. "It was nice of you to invite all the tenants."

"I just hope Michael thinks so. I issued the invitation when I still had my own place."

"Which is now empty. Does Michael plan on renting it out to someone else now?"

"I don't know. We haven't had time to talk about it. Listen, before I forget, I wanted to tell you that I'm delighted that Tyrone was able to make it here today. Finally I get to meet him after just hearing about him."

"He's mighty fine, isn't he?" Keisha said proudly.

Brett nodded. In contrast to his outgoing and direct wife, Tyrone was quiet and more introverted. He seemed to be having a good time talking to Michael about the recent football play-off games.

Meanwhile, Frieda and Consuela were having a good time fussing over Hope, who was delighting in all the attention. Consuela had made a little Santa Claus cap for

Hope. The baby loved playing peek-a-boo with it, tugging the red cap over her eyes, chuckling to herself, and then pushing it back up again. In honor of the party, Brett had dressed the little girl in one of the adorable frilly dresses Consuela's daughter had lent her. This one was pink, and had little flowers embroidered on the collar.

So far, Hope hadn't spit anything on the outfit, but from experience, Brett knew that wouldn't last long. Thank heavens all the clothes were washable, her own included.

Tired of the black leggings she'd been wearing so much over the past few weeks, today Brett was wearing jeans and a denim shirt along with the colorful red vest that Michael's parents had given her Christmas Eve.

Mr. Stephanopolis joined them at the buffet table just as Keisha was saying, "We've been invited to a Kwansa celebration later today."

"I never did understand why you'd want to celebrate Kansas," he declared.

"Who's talking about Kansas?" Keisha retorted.

"You were."

"Kwansa not Kansas," Brett said, sharing a smile with Keisha as Mr. Stephanopolis tapped his hearing aid with an impatient finger.

"And it's meant to celebrate a sense of family and community as well as our ethnic history," Keisha added.

"Those are important things," he agreed. "That makes more sense. Here all this time I been thinking it was Kansas. I gotta go tell the wife. I love it when I know something she doesn't. Excuse me, ladies."

Brett and Keisha tried stifling their laughter in their glasses of sparkling grape juice. All Brett ended up doing was getting bubbles up her nose. Michael arrived in time to pound her on the back as she had a coughing fit. She noticed he continued his ongoing football conversation with Tyrone without missing a beat as he absently patted her on the shoulder before reaching around her for some cookies.

She was tempted to do something outrageous, like cupping Michael's denim-clad derriere within her hand and borrowing Keisha's expression of "mighty fine." Instead she held her tongue, even though she'd rather have swirled it around her husband's full lower lip.

As the men drifted off, Keisha said, "You got it bad, girl!"

"Yeah, I know," Brett said with a sigh. "Does it really show?"

"You was drooling over your man the way that baby drools over practically everything."

"I was not!" Brett denied.

Keisha just grinned and handed Brett a paper napkin with holiday greetings on it.

The arrival of Michael's family was a welcome diversion. Brett had invited them but wasn't sure if they'd come. She was glad they did. Maria brought poppy-seed cookies and Konrad was the hit of the party with his stories about their Pacific Rim cruise.

Only one thing prevented the gathering from being perfect, and that was the realization that although Brett had fallen in love with Michael, he didn't feel the same way about her.

She tried to hide her inner yearning when looking at Michael as he proudly showed off Hope, but apparently she hadn't done a very good job because her new mother-in-law patted her on the shoulder and softly said, "Don't you go worrying about adopting that little baby. Things will work out, you'll see. Don't give up hope."


"Singing in the beans, I'm singing in the beans...." Brett sang her own lyrics to the tune of "Singing in the Rain" as she fed Hope dinner of vegetable pasta.

Actually it was a cooperative operation, with the little girl contributing by putting individual strands of cut spaghetti in her own mouth as well as trying to put one in Brett's mouth every so often. When she succeeded, the baby got so excited she grabbed spaghetti in both hands and tossed it to the winds. Not exactly what Brett had had in mind when she took the leftover spaghetti from last night's dinner, minus any sauce, out of the fridge.

"'The more your baby is permitted to help at mealtime, the faster she will learn to eat on her own,'" Brett quoted from one of the books she'd read, reminding herself why she was going through this messy and time-consuming operation as she peeled sticky spaghetti off her forehead. The rain slicker helped, although the first time she'd put on the yellow rain gear to feed Hope, Brett felt like Gene Kelly in the famous musical—hence her own vegetable rendition of the song.

Successive feedings had provided her with more ideas— like spreading newspapers under the high chair during mealtime.

Completely unrepentant of the mess she was making, Hope gleefully bounced in her high chair while babbling "ga-ga-ga."

As Brett leaned down to check out a full-page sale ad at a local hardware store, the baby suddenly pounded on the high-chair tray and said, "Maa-maa!" Out of the corner of her eye, Brett saw the little girl pointing at her.

Brett straightened so fast she almost got whiplash. Her shriek of excitement made Michael race into the kitchen so fast his socks slid across the linoleum floor.

"What's wrong?" he demanded as he saw tears in Brett's eyes.

"She called me Mommy," Brett said in awe. "Well, actually she called me Mama."

"Are you sure she wasn't just saying 'ga-ga' like she does?"

"This was definitely 'mama.' And she pointed right at me. Say it again, Hope."

Instead she said "Daaa-daaa!"

"The kid can talk!" he shouted, as thrilled as Brett had been. "Wait a second, I've got to get this on videotape. Don't move," he told Brett and Hope as he rushed into the other room to get the video camera. "Okay, let me get this thing turned on. Okay, stinky britches..."

"She's going to see this when she's twenty," Brett reminded him.

"Say it again, honey," he said.

"Say what, sweetie pie?" Brett replied with a sassy grin.

"Very funny." He paused to zoom in on Brett's face, unable to resist trying to capture the way she glowed, before aiming the camera at Hope again. "Come on, Hope. Say 'da-da' again. You can do it."

The baby did it all right, picking up several pieces of spaghetti and hurling them straight at the camera lens, chortling with satisfaction at her own cleverness.

"Just for that I'm going to call you stinky britches until you are twenty-one," Michael told her, turning the camera around to study the damage.

"Did you want some marinara sauce to go with that pasta?" Brett asked him in her best waitress voice while handing him a cloth to wipe the lens.

"Never irritate a man with a camera," Brett told Hope before removing any further edible projectiles from the baby's reach.

"Ma-ma," Hope said, her baby voice filled with overtones of complaint. "Ma-ma-ma-ma-ma, ga-ga-ga-ba-ga!" she gurgled, waving her hands at Brett as if to get her attention.

The little girl already had Brett's attention. Michael's attention was focused on the two of them through the viewfinder of his video camera. As he filmed them, he chalked up the strange tug on his heart to something he'd eaten.

"It's been quite a night," Brett said as she joined him in the living room.

"We need a couch," he declared.

She blinked at him. "What brought that on?"

He shrugged, not about to tell her that it was more difficult to "make out" in a recliner than it was on a couch. More difficult but not impossible, he decided, eyeing her. She'd changed from her leggings and sweatshirt into a skirt—a very *short* suede skirt.

The color, a deep turquoise, suited her. The mohair cropped cardigan she wore with it made him itch to reach out to test its softness. He was also dying to find out if she was wearing anything underneath, because it sure didn't look like it. The top button was undone and all he saw below it was skin. Her skin, creamy and soft, as lustrous as the single strand of pearls she wore, their demureness a direct contrast to the rest of her outfit.

He licked his lips, hoping he wasn't openly smacking them. She looked delicious.

She had stockings on beneath her skirt, because he could see the shimmer on her lovely legs as she seductively sauntered closer. Since when had she sauntered like a siren? Lord, he'd never seen such sexy ankles! Hell, he'd never even *seen* her ankles before—she was always wearing boots or athletic shoes. Now she wore heels and they made her legs look like they went on forever, from slim ankle to seductive thigh. Lots of thigh!

Michael wiped his brow and reached for the remote control, hitting the volume button by mistake.

"Three, two, one," the announcer said as the screen displayed the illuminated ball at Times Square. "Happy New Year, everybody!"

Michael didn't care about *every* body, he only cared about Brett's.

"Are you warm?" she asked. "I am," she noted, opening another button and displaying the shadowy valley between her breasts. "It must be because of those hot cinnamon rolls I just baked. The oven warmed things up."

*She* was warming things up, he thought to himself, unable to take his eyes from that vee of skin showing between her fuzzy sweater.

Noticing his interest, Brett nervously took a deep breath and told herself not to chicken out now. She'd been planning this seduction for almost a week—the miniskirt; the return of her miracle bra . . . and nothing else . . . under the cardigan; the erotic rip-away black-lace panties she was wearing, and last but not least, the hot cinnamon rolls. Just yesterday she'd heard on the local news that a Chicago research scientist had discovered that the scent that aroused men the most wasn't musk or anything else you could buy in a bottle. It was the smell of hot cinnamon rolls.

Presto, Brett had added baking to her battle plan. She'd even dabbed a touch of cinnamon behind each ear, just to be sure.

Michael, poor sexy soul, looked like a man besieged. He was wearing dark slacks and a white shirt. She didn't aim on him wearing them long.

"Ah . . ." He cleared his throat and started again. "I . . . ah . . . never heard of baking cinnamon rolls for the holiday. . . . Have I told you how we celebrate *Szilveszter?*"

"Who is Silvester?"

"Not a who, a what. It's New Year's Eve. And we always celebrated the holiday with drinking, dancing and music and eating *virsli* at the stroke of midnight."

"What's *virsli?*"

"Sausage, sort of."

She wrinkled her nose. "I'm not keen on that part, but the rest sounds good. I've got some champagne chilling in the fridge."

Michael thought the only way to cool his overheated blood was for *him* to chill in the fridge.

She came back from the kitchen with two champagne glasses in one hand and the bottle in the other. "I looked out the kitchen window and it's really snowing hard out there. It's a good thing we're staying home tonight. Here, would you pop the cork for me?"

He swallowed, unsettled by the way the overhead kitchen light had backlit her entire body, creating a repeat of the magical image he'd seen when he'd first opened the Rom box. She looked like an angel. And he had yet to find the box, which had been missing since the day after she'd moved in.

"Michael?" Brett repeated. "The bottle? Can you open it?"

"Oh, right. Sure."

Aiming the bottle in the corner, he almost knocked the star off the small Christmas tree on Brett's scarred pine dining table with the cork that came flying out of the bottle.

"Nice shot," she said with a grin. "I guess we really should wait to make a toast until midnight, but there's no reason we can't sample the bubbly now, right?"

Nodding, he poured himself a glass and gulped it in one go and then had to watch while Brett daintily sipped hers, driving him crazy with the sultry sheen on her luscious lips.

"Now all we need is music and dancing," she murmured before taking the remote control. She switched channels to a black-and-white movie classic, *Top Hat*. Fred and Ginger were dancing and it was magic.

"I always wanted to learn to dance like that," she said somewhat wistfully.

"I can teach you," he replied, setting down their drinks and taking her in his arms before she could say no.

They might not have tripped the light fantastic quite as nimbly as Fred and Ginger, but with her right hand in Michael's and her left hand poised upon his shoulder, Brett felt every bit as light on her feet as the legendary dancers. Of course, the fact that she was in Michael's arms was the real reason for this blissful sensation of floating inches above the ground. Being held this close to him was more intoxicating than an entire case of the world's best champagne.

Once the dance was over, the movie characters went on to the next scene. Scooping up the remote control with his right hand, Michael smoothly hit the Off button even as he lowered his mouth to hers for a kiss that was a merging of souls as well as lips. He practiced the subtle art of seduction, captivating her with the thrust of his tongue.

Feeling her knees weakening, she slid her hands around his neck, dragging her fingers through his dark hair. She was delighted by the rough silkiness of it. Murmuring her name, and incorporating it in their kiss, Michael tugged her even closer.

The hem of her cardigan had lifted when her arms had, leaving a patch around her middle bare to his avid explorations. He slid his hand from the small of her back up beneath the mohair material, testing his theory that she wasn't wearing much underneath. He felt the constricting band of her bra and sought to remove it, but the back was smooth—it must have a front fastener.

Temporarily diverted, Michael slid his hand down her back, appreciating the velvety texture of her suede skirt as he cupped her derriere before sliding lower, to steal beneath her skirt, lifting it as he moved his hand back up until he encountered the elastic top of her thigh-high stockings.

By now, Brett was completely consumed with her need for him. Judging by the way he rubbed against her, she knew he felt the same. There was no time for words as they sank to the floor.

He rested atop her so that they were pressed together from shoulder to hip. The electrifying contact was made even more intimate when he wedged his leg between hers. She was on fire. He'd incited a riot of pleasure within her and the craving for consummation was so intense there was no time to think, only to act.

She reached for the zip on his slacks as he fumbled with the buttons on her cardigan. Once her sweater was undone, he quickly dispatched the front fastening of her bra in order to cup her small breasts in the palm of his hands. Before self-consciousness could take hold of her, Michael had lowered his head. His lips closed around the rosy crest, tugging her swiftly, sweetly into his mouth. He drove her to a higher level of desire with every hot, wet, velvety stroke of his tongue.

He was so painfully gentle and deliciously demanding that Brett didn't care that they were lying on the dhurrie rug in the middle of the living room floor. She felt as if the world were going to explode any second and she needed him within her... *now!*

When his hand glided beneath her panties to caress her moist warmth with skillful wickedness, she knew she couldn't wait a moment longer. Guiding his hand to the narrow sides of her underwear, she whispered, "Rip them off."

He did. She helped him shove his underwear out of the way and in doing so, her elbow inadvertently hit the remote control button. The large TV screen blinked on, televising Chicago's countdown.

Michael came to her, surging into her as the count began.

*"Ten... nine... eight..."*

His heated thrusts coincided with each slipping second.

"*Seven...six...five...*"

Brett gasped with pleasure as the tension mounted.

"*Four...three...two...*"

She raised her hips to take him more fully within her.

"*...one...*"

"Yes!" Brett cried as the first clenching ripples of satisfaction shot through her. "Yes, yes, yes!"

"*Happy New Year!*"

Her inner muscles tightened around him as she climaxed. The TV was abruptly silenced and the room was instead filled with the sound of her breathy moans of joy and his shout of pleasure as he joined her in the culmination of ecstasy that ended with him stiffening and then collapsing in her arms.

When Brett next opened her eyes, she saw fireworks. It took her a second to realize the chromatic display was on TV. Closing her eyes, she ran her hand over his bare back. He had his face buried in the crook of her shoulder. She threaded her hand through his dark hair, fascinated by the vibrant thickness of it.

When he finally leaned away from her, he gave her that rare, devilish, slow grin of his before saying, "That was better than eating *virsli.*"

"I should hope so," she said with a demure smile.

"We went a little crazy," he murmured.

"Mmm-hmm," she agreed.

"You still have your clothes on."

"Not all of them."

"Did I hurt you?"

She shook her head. "Did I hurt *you?*" she inquired with a sassy smile.

"You may have put your mark on me here or there," he replied, flexed his back muscles beneath her fingertips.

"Only here or there?"

"Everywhere."

"You're an amazing... dancer, Mr. Janos."

"So are you, Mrs. Janos. Are you ready for another lesson?"

She let her smile speak for her.

Getting to his feet, he held out his hand to her. Taking it, she let out a surprised squeal as he tugged her up right into his arms.

"There you go, sweeping me off my feet again," she said with delight.

"This time we're going to go slow," he stated as he walked into his bedroom. Setting her in the middle of his tousled sheets, he muttered, "You drive me crazy when you do that."

"What?" she asked in husky surprise. "What did I do?"

"This." Leaning forward on both hands, he ran his tongue around her upper lip, mimicking her nervous action of a moment ago.

This time their kiss was slowly evocative and darkly erotic. He kissed her as if he had all the time in the world, as if he were writing a ten-volume treatise on every detail of her mouth. He took his sweet time, leisurely exploring all the delicate unexpected places—the curving slope of the roof of her mouth, the delicious fullness of her lower lip, the demure curve of her upper lip. Each caress was richly extravagant.

He gave the same attention to detail to each inch of creamy skin he revealed as he removed every stitch of her clothing. First he grazed her with the merest brush of his fingertips. Then he repeated his explorations with his bold mouth and seductive tongue—moving from the enticing warmth at the base of her throat, down over her creamy breasts. He skimmed her navel before shifting his attentions even lower. There he paused to spread his heated message of impassioned need.

At the first forbidden contact, she gasped at the bolt of ecstasy that shot through her with that hot, wet touch.

Lifting his head, he gave her a devilish smile. "Ah, you like that, hmm?"

Tethering her with his arm across her waist, he resumed his most intimate of kisses.

Needing to hold onto something as hard-edged pleasure clenched its delicate hold on her, Brett grasped the rungs of the bed's brass headboard. The cold metal contrasted with the fiery shivers that had her bucking beneath him. Squeezing her eyes closed, she shattered into a million pieces, hazily thinking she'd never felt such pleasure in her entire life, only to have him repeat his creative seduction. Seconds later, she convulsed around his teasing fingers as he kissed his way back up her body.

Abandoning the anchor of the headboard, she blindly reached for him.

Unable to hold back a moment longer, Michael levered himself into readiness before slowly burying himself deep within her. He groaned in ecstasy as he felt the rippling bliss of her inner muscles clenching around him. Rocking against her, his well-intentioned slow seduction became a rapid surge of motion that ended in his climax and her smile of utter satisfaction.

When Michael finally returned to this planet, the first thing he saw was the Rom box, sitting on top of his dresser across from the bed, the metal glowing in the darkness.

Turning her head, Brett noticed it, too.

"I guess that box worked like a charm after all," he murmured.

# Nine

"What's that supposed to mean?" Brett said.

"Nothing. Forget it."

"No way." She sat up in bed, forgetting for a moment that she wasn't wearing anything before belatedly making a hasty grab for the top sheet and tucking it under her arms as she turned to face Michael. "I thought you said that Rom box was missing."

"I thought it was."

"Then how did it get on your dresser?"

"I don't know."

"That box seems to be very mysterious," she noted suspiciously. "Now that I think about it, I seem to recall your dad saying something..." Pausing, Brett concentrated. "I remember now. When you first told him we were married, he said something about the box being responsible. Why would he think that?"

Michael could tell by the look on her face that she wasn't going to let this subject go until she got some answers.

Sighing, he put an arm around her and tugged her closer. At least he could hold her while telling her about the supposedly magical Rom box. "Now don't laugh, but family legend has it that the box has a love charm cast on it."

Brett wasn't laughing. Instead a chill ran up her bare spine as it occurred to her that a love charm actually might explain quite a lot. It might explain why a man like Michael, who'd been skillful at avoiding what he'd apparently once described as the "chains of matrimony" had suddenly changed his mind and decided to get married . . . to save a foundling child abandoned in his building. Since Brett often thought with her heart instead of her head, this behavior wasn't all that out of place for her. But from what she knew of Michael and his past, it was *not* a behavioral trademark of his.

Was it possible that Michael hadn't acted out of his own free will, but had been "charmed" into marrying her?

"What exactly is this love charm supposed to do?"

"Supposedly you'll 'find love where you look for it.'"

"Look for it how?"

"Well, the legend claims that you'll find love with the first person of the opposite sex you see after opening the box."

"And you opened that box while I was at your place fixing your oven that first day," she said slowly.

"And it works like a charm now."

"The box or the oven?"

"I was referring to the oven. I don't believe in magic," Michael declared.

"Your father certainly believes in it. He thinks that's why we got married."

"What does it matter what my father thinks?"

"It matters because you were raised by your father. Some of his beliefs are bound to have rubbed off on you, whether you want to admit it or not," she said, her mind racing a mile a minute.

She supposed the sensible thing to do would be to shrug the legend off as nothing more than a Gypsy superstition. But what if there *was* something to the story? Brett certainly hadn't experienced much magic in her own life, so she was no expert in such matters. After all, who would have thought that cinnamon rolls would arouse a man? It was true that facts could be stranger than fiction.

*Great,* she thought to herself. *Michael made love to me because of cinnamon rolls and married me because of a Gypsy curse. I'm really batting a thousand here.*

Now that she thought about it, some pretty strange things had been happening lately—like those black silk boxer shorts showing up under the Christmas tree. Or what about Michael's sudden development of "baby" skills, when by his own admission they'd always screamed around him before? And then there was the way she felt when Michael even so much as looked at her...she'd used the term "magical" in her own mind a number of times. Was it really so strange to think she and Michael had been "charmed"?

Well, okay, so it was a little unusual. Not exactly your run of the mill experience. She could just see herself asking Father Lynden for advice. "You see, there's this Gypsy love charm that's been cast on me...."

Yeah, right.

"You're awfully quiet," Michael noted in concern, having learned from experience that when Brett got quiet it was time to get worried.

"Let's just say that I think this family legend of yours might explain a lot of what's happened in our relationship."

"Like what?"

"Like this inflammatory thing between us."

"This inflammatory thing?" he murmured huskily, taking her hand and placing it around his throbbing arousal.

In a fiery instant, Brett's thoughts and worries went up in smoke. So did Michael, as she caressed him with sultry enchantment.

After they'd made love, and while they lay exhausted in each other's arms, Brett couldn't help brooding about the niggling possibility that something was going on here.

She didn't realize she'd spoken her words aloud until Michael murmured, "Nothing's going on. Not until I get some energy back. Maybe then . . ."

"I was talking about the love spell," she said.

"I told you I don't believe in that stuff."

"Yeah, well, the power of suggestion is an incredible thing. People who claim they don't believe in voodoo can still can be affected by spells simply by the power of suggestion. Believe me, after all the psychology courses I've had, I know how powerful the mind can be."

"So what are you saying? That I didn't marry you of my own free will?"

"You have to admit that our . . . relationship hasn't exactly been a normal one."

"Just because there's an intense physical attraction between us, that doesn't mean anything else is going on. . . . What?" he said, seeing the look on her face.

"I think I hear Hope crying." Tossing aside the covers, Brett grabbed the nearest piece of clothing at hand—his white shirt—and pulled it around her. "I'll just go check on her. No, don't get up. I'll take care of this."

She hurried out of the room, biting her lower lip to keep from crying. What she considered to be love, Michael considered to be "an intense physical attraction" and nothing else. Even after they'd made love. Well, she'd made love to him. He'd apparently just had sex with her.

In the bedroom she shared with Hope, Brett stared down at the sleeping infant, smoothing the little girl's silky head with her trembling fingers and willing the tears not to fall.

"Why can't you just be satisfied with the way things are?" Brett remembered one of her foster parents asking her. "Why do you always have to want something more?"

Right now the "something more" Brett wanted was Michael's love.

"It is good luck to serve pork on New Year's Day," Konrad was telling Brett the next afternoon as they sat down to a dinner of pork roast, boiled new potatoes and asparagus at Michael's parents' house.

"Good luck, but bad for the arteries," was his mother's annual reply.

But Michael's attention wasn't on his parents' fond bickering, it was on Brett. While Brett had been outwardly cheerful since they'd arrived, he sensed her pulling away from him, focusing her attention on Hope and practically ignoring him. It was the damn box's fault!

Michael knew it would do no good enlisting his parents' help. His father was convinced Rom magic had brought Michael and Brett together, that theirs was a love match helped along by a powerful dose of a centuries-old love spell. Michael wished he'd never mentioned the stupid box to Brett. He'd certainly never expected her to take the family legend so seriously. Did she honestly think any power of suggestion was strong enough to make him marry her if he hadn't wanted to?

Michael's exact reasons for marrying Brett weren't ones he cared to dwell on at the moment, however. Instead, he preferred to focus on the erotic memories of making love to Brett and her incredible response. He wasn't going to have her pull away from him now. He'd prove to her how much he wanted her. After all, he'd never courted her, had never even dated her before they'd gotten married. Perhaps he'd been too businesslike and practical at first.

But there was no need for that now. He had plenty of romance in his soul; he had Rom blood for God's sake. No one else was as romantic as the Rom, particularly a Hungarian Rom. He'd show her how much he wanted her, starting tonight.

As they got ready for bed that night, Brett considered telling Michael she would be sleeping in her own bed, before deciding it was no good cutting off her nose to spite her face. If chemistry was all he felt, she'd stop wishing for the moon and settle for what she had. It wasn't as if what they'd shared last night hadn't been downright awesome. Maybe love would grow. . . .

Damn, it was hard for her to give up hope. It seemed to have become second nature to her.

Today's newly fallen snow, combined with its being the first day of the new year, had gotten her to thinking about new beginnings, about possibilities. But it was a future filled with land mines, and fraught with emotional danger. Brett had always been able to say goodbye before, to let go as those she cared about moved on. She didn't know if she'd be able to do that with Michael. If there came a time when he realized how impulsively he'd entered into this marriage, and he decided he wanted more—wanted children of his own—Brett didn't know if she'd have the strength to let him go. And she hated that weakness in herself.

Michael ended up taking matters into his own hands—by moving her clothes to his closet while she dashed down to the basement to bring up a load of wash she'd left in the dryer. She came back upstairs to find him taking the final armload of her stuff into "their" room.

"I set up the baby monitor my folks gave us for Christmas in here too, on the bedside table, so you'd be able to hear Hope if she cries in the night," Michael told Brett, looking at her with such a look of expectant pleasure that she didn't have the heart to reprimand him for not asking her about the move first. After all, they were husband and wife now.

In the end, Brett's number-one New Year's resolution was to be happy with the miracles she had—a darling baby and a husband, both of whom she loved—and not worry how she got them or how she'd manage if she lost them.

The next few weeks sped by, hurried along by the fact that Brett started her class at Loyola as well as continuing her repairs on the building. She also had her hands full taking care of a very active Hope. And on those nights when they weren't interrupted by the baby's crying, Brett made love with her husband, enjoying the creativity of his lovemaking, but out of self-preservation, holding a part of herself—her heart—back.

As if sensing that, Michael had become a man with a mission. And that mission seemed to be to capture her heart.

She'd never seen Michael bent on seduction. He was more powerful than any Gypsy magic could be. He pursued her with a brooding intensity that was difficult if not impossible to resist.

Take today, for example. Some men sent roses. Not Michael. He had a heart-shaped box delivered, filled with . . . a dozen acorns.

She wondered if he was telling her she was a few acorns short of an oak tree, as in not fully compos mentis, when she found the note inside that said "To the Rom, acorns are tokens of desire."

Brett fingered the paper, tracing the dramatic flare of Michael's handwriting. This was the first note he'd ever written to her. The one that said "Buy milk and eggs," which he'd left on the fridge hadn't counted, in her view.

So Michael had moved from chemistry to desire. Was that an upward move? Or a linear one?

While Brett had protectively sequestered her heart away, her body had a mind of its own and enjoyed the fiery lovemaking she shared with Michael as if there were no tomorrow. In fact, they hadn't talked much about the future . . .

The ringing phone interrupted her thoughts. "Hello?"

"I need you to come to my office today," Michael said in a businesslike tone of voice. "Can you get here by one o'clock?"

"What's this about?" she asked.

"Bring Hope."

"Why? Is something wrong?"

"No. I just need you to stop by. Consider it your chance to check out Lorraine personally."

Lorraine was his secretary, and Michael had mentioned her several times over the past few weeks. It was the first time he'd talked about his work. Actually he still hadn't talked about his *work* as much as his secretary—who was the model of efficient perfection according to him. When Brett had casually asked, he hadn't given her any physical details or even Lorraine's age.

"I have better things to do than check out your secretary," Brett told him. "That energy-efficient thermostat needs to be installed on the boiler."

"I really need you to stop by," Michael said in his most coaxing voice, the one that would convince a vegetarian to eat red meat.

She gave in. "All right, I'll be there. But I can't stay long."

Brett dressed carefully. Actually, her choice of attire was limited, as all of her leggings and jeans seemed to have mysteriously disappeared into the wash. That's what she got for taking Michael up on his offer to do the laundry. The wool tweed skirt she wore was nice and long for the cold weather outside. There wasn't much snow left on the ground, so her hiking boots would do fine. An Irish fisherman's sweater lent the outfit a funky look. She'd never make glamorous, so funky would have to do. She did remember to put on lipstick and earrings before she left the house, however.

Hope looked adorable in the denim overalls she wore under the snowsuit, which fit her a little better than it had the month before.

They got to Michael's northside office a little after one, to find Lorraine had gone out to lunch.

"She's sorry she missed you," Michael said as he took Hope from Brett's arms.

"Yeah, I'll bet," Brett muttered.

"But she promised her granddaughter she'd meet her for lunch."

"Granddaughter?"

"Yeah, didn't I tell you? Lorraine has four grandchildren. One is in college now."

Brett relaxed a little. "Hope, this is where your daddy tracks down criminals," she told the little girl as she undid her snowsuit.

"You make me sound like Batman," Michael stated dryly.

"You two do share a similar dark personality."

"Gee, thanks."

"You're welcome." She wasn't about to tell him that on him, dark and brooding looked good. "So what was so important that I had to come rushing down here? Is it that social worker? Has she contacted you or anything?"

"No. She stopped by my office before we were married, but I haven't heard from her lately."

"What! I didn't know she'd come by to see you. Why didn't you tell me this before?"

"Because I didn't want to worry you."

"And what else haven't you told me in the name of not wanting to worry me?"

"Hmm, I can't think of anything except for the fact that when you put your hands on your hips that way I want to rip your clothes off and make love to you, regardless of where we are. Right here, in my office, on my desk . . ."

"Stop that." She picked up a file folder off his desk and started fanning her face with it. "Go on about the social worker."

"She stopped by to ask me about the mystery baby, as she called her." Michael juggled Hope on his hip as he spoke.

"She knows Hope is a girl?"

"She overheard that when she heard my friend from the police department talking to me. The woman reminded me of a bulldog. I think I'm going to have to create a paper trail to make her happy," he muttered half under his breath.

"What do you mean a paper trail?"

"Create a paper trail for that imaginary friend of yours who left her baby with you."

"You're talking about falsifying records?"

"If necessary."

"I can't let you do that," Brett protested. "It's too big a risk for you."

"I'm prepared to fight for my family, if it comes to that. I know what I'm doing. But we won't be able to adopt Hope without having some kind of substantiating paperwork to give the court."

"You can't give a court falsified records. You could end up in jail!"

"You have a better idea?"

"Not yet. But I can certainly see lots of trouble with your plan. What if Hope's mother comes back?"

"If she hasn't shown up yet, it's doubtful she will."

"Doubtful maybe, but not impossible."

"You haven't had any more nightmares about someone taking the baby, have you?"

Brett shook her head while Hope started fussing, tired of the adults talking over her head and not including her.

"Aha, I hear the sound of an unhappy camper," Gaylynn announced as she entered the office. "I guess this is my cue to take her off your hands for a bit, hmm?" Holding out her arms for the little girl, Gaylynn took her from Michael. Delighted that someone was finally paying attention to her, Hope tugged on Gaylynn's shoulder-length hair. "Now, kiddo, you don't want your aunt to go bald, do you?" she demanded, gently opening the little girl's clenched fist and then pressing smacking kisses on her little palm. Hope chortled in delight.

"I didn't expect to see you here, Gaylynn," Brett noted. "Isn't today a school day?"

"School is closed for Martin Luther King's birthday. I'm ahead of schedule with report cards, which means I get to spend some time with my favorite niece, if that's okay with you?"

"Sure it is," Michael said while Brett frowned at him suspiciously.

"I left the basket on your secretary's desk," Gaylynn said as she bustled Hope back into her snowsuit. "Expect us back in about two hours."

"Fine, thanks."

"What's going on here?" Brett demanded of Michael once his sister had left.

"A seduction," Michael told her, closing the door.

Brett heard the click as he locked the door.

"You tricked me into coming down here so you . . ."

"Could have my wicked way with you," he completed for her. "Guilty as charged."

"I can't believe you did this."

"Believe it." He spread out a thin blanket on the floor. Kneeling down on it, he proceeded to open up the picnic basket he'd picked up from his secretary's desk, where Gaylynn had left it. "Yes, we have the best that Meli's Deli has to offer. We've got roast beef or Reuben here. Which would you prefer?"

"I'd prefer to know why you're doing this."

"I already told you."

"What do you hope to accomplish?" Seeing his look, she blushed. "Aside from—" she wiggled her hand "—that."

"*That* is enough to bring a grown man to his knees," he noted dryly, holding out one hand to her as he knelt on the floor. "Why don't you kick off your boots and join me down here?"

She did, even while asking, "What about your secretary? Won't she be coming back from lunch soon?"

"I gave her the afternoon off," he replied, biting into a Reuben sandwich as he gave her the roast beef one.

"The afternoon off? Don't you have work to do?" she said, a bit aggravated by the fact that he always seemed to get his way.

"I'm taking a break."

"You know, you never talk to me about your work. Why is that?"

"You distract me. And my work isn't all that interesting."

"Corporate security work isn't interesting?"

"Do you really want to have a discussion about the fine points of white-collar crime?" he inquired wryly.

"I guess not. Maybe it would be better if we discussed a logical course of action for our plans to adopt Hope."

They did talk about several options, while enjoying the lunch Michael had provided and his sister had picked up for him. Brett didn't even realize he was tempting her with samples of finger food until his fingers brushed her lips for the fifth time in as many minutes.

"You know you haven't been acting at all like yourself lately," she commented. "Maybe we should talk to your father about that box. The spell might be getting stronger or something."

Michael felt like rolling his eyes in exasperation. "Fine, if you believe in Rom magic boxes, then perhaps I should practice another bit of popular folklore. Give me your hand."

"Why?"

"Just give it to me." Taking her hand in his, he turned it over so that he could see her palm. "It's time for me to do a little Gypsy fortune-telling."

"I thought you told me they prefer to be called Rom. And I read that fortune-telling is never done by men."

He looked at her in surprise. "How do you know that?"

She shrugged self-consciously. "I slipped a book about Gypsy legends in with those baby care books I checked out of the library."

"Yeah, well, I've been Americanized." He wasn't about to admit that he'd bought a book on fortune-telling from the bookstore down the street. "Now shush, I'm concentrating."

Brett wasn't able to concentrate or even think at all, not with his fingertip leisurely trailing over the sensitive heart of her palm. Lordy, it was an incredibly sexy feeling! Just from him touching her hand? Wow...

"I'll start with the basics," Michael murmured in that dark, rich voice of his. "This one here near the base of your thumb is your life line. Ah, very nice. Long, narrow, deep and completely encircling the Mount of Venus, which represents the pleasures of the senses."

She should have snatched her hand away at that point. But apparently she liked pleasuring her senses a little too much, because she couldn't work up the willpower to put a halt to his wickedly delightful seduction.

"And this one going right across your palm in the middle here is the line that rules your head," he murmured.

"I'll bet it's cracked," she muttered. "Denoting muddled thinking."

"On the contrary, the line is even and narrow, showing excellent judgment and a strong will."

If she had excellent judgment she wouldn't be sitting with him on the floor of his office, nearly panting at the shivery delight the merest stroke of her life line provoked. Each sliding caress left a gossamer trail of tingling awareness behind.

"And last but not least is your heart line." Michael lifted his eyes to stare directly into hers. "Ah, I see a tall dark handsome stranger coming into your life."

"Yeah, I think he's in my Developmental Psych class at Loyola."

Michael frowned fiercely and glared at her.

She responded by batting her eyelashes at him.

"The longer the heart line, the more ideal the love," he said.

"*Ideal* meaning all in my mind and having nothing to do with reality, right?"

"And this is the mouth line," he said. "See how wide it is? Indicating a woman who talks too much."

"Get out of here! There's no such thing as a mouth line. Is there?"

He gave her one of his slow smiles. This time, her attempt to keep a perspective on things by using her sense of humor as a defense died a quick death. She would have been fine, if he hadn't brought her hand to his lips. His wicked eyes never left hers as he flicked his tongue over the back of her knuckles before darting into the sensitized valley between her fingers.

She would have melted there and then, tumbling back onto the small blanket and tugging him down after her, but then they both would have ended up in the vegetable dip.

"Damn, I wish I had a couch in here," he muttered through her fingers, nipping them with his white teeth before hauling her to him and kissing her.

"You should have planned ahead," she whispered against his mouth.

"I've got an idea...." Leaping to his feet, he tugged her up to stand beside him.

Before she could speak, he was kissing her once more. With teasing smacks, gentle nibbles and hungry swirls of his tongue he urged her backwards until her bottom bumped into the top of his desk. Putting his hands on her waist, he picked her up and set her on the flat surface. Nudging her legs apart, he moved closer, tugging her flush against him, so that his erection was pressed to her.

"Is that an acorn in your pocket or are you just glad to see me?" she saucily paraphrased Mae West.

"Where are those rip-away panties when a man needs them?" he muttered as he slid his hands beneath her skirt and grappled with her sturdy cotton underwear.

She nibbled on his ear until he finally disposed of her panties, tossing them over his shoulder in triumph. The next move was hers as she undid the fastening on his pants, brushing the back of her fingers against him as she slowly lowered the zipper's metal tab. He was wearing the black silk boxer shorts she'd gotten for him.

When she freed him from its silky confines, his throbbing manhood eagerly leapt to life in her hand.

"Who's doing the seducing here?" he demanded huskily, as she caressed him with gentle strokes.

"So far all I've heard is talk, not much action," she purred.

"How's this for action?" he growled, clearing the top of his desk with one sweep of his hand and lowering her onto it until the tilt of her hips was perfect for their joining. He came to her swiftly, her knees bracketing his hips. Their bodies slipped into an erotic rhythm as he moved against her with tight urgency and exquisite sureness. Fiery bliss shimmered and rippled through her, the propulsive motion lifting her to a dizzying peak of rapture.

Afterwards, once she'd regained the ability to breath and speak, she muttered, "We've definitely had some kind of spell cast on us. There's no other explanation for what just happened."

"Sure there is."

"Yeah, I know you think it's just chemistry," she said as she sat up and restored order to her mussed clothing.

"Chemistry is a powerful thing."

So is love, she wanted to shout. But the words froze in her throat as the hurtful phrases from her past rose in her mind to taunt her:

*Don't be a nuisance, Brett.*
*Why do you always have to want more?*
*I need a woman who can be a real wife.*


"Man, will you look at that kid go?" Michael marveled as Hope crawled across the floor.

It was early February and Hope was eight months old. They'd survived her first cold and her second tooth. They'd seen her grow and develop into a perpetual-motion machine, capable of wearing out even the sturdiest adults.

Other than that one relapse in Michael's office, Brett had kept her New Year's resolution of appreciating what she had while acknowledging that there was no controlling the inner longings of her heart. Some days she pretended Michael loved her and that he just couldn't say the words. Some days it was enough.

Brett watched Michael as he watched Hope's movements in awed amusement. "She's like one of those wind-up toys that keeps going until it runs into something solid. Then you just pick it up and aim it in the opposite direction," he said, doing just that as Hope got close to the base

of his rack stereo system. He'd long since moved everything above baby-reaching level.

"Oh-oh, she's heading for your newspaper," Brett
warned him. Hope had developed a curiosity about everything. She had a particular fondness for paper.

"I think she reads the thing when we're not looking,"
he claimed.

"She's in her reach-and-explore phase," Brett said.

"Search-and-destroy, you mean," he replied as Hope
crumpled the headlines before he removed the *Tribune*
from her reach.

"Speaking of searching, have you heard any more about
that social worker?" Brett asked.

"As a matter of fact, I got a call from my buddy this
afternoon. Strangest thing, the woman decided to take an
early retirement. Last time he saw her, right before she left,
she acted like she'd never heard of the 'mystery baby' she'd
been bugging him about." As he spoke, Michael eyed the
Rom box, now stored on top of the bookcase, suspiciously. If he were a superstitious man, he might think
there really *was* some kind of magic going on here. Thank
heavens he was the logical type.

"She's gone? That's a relief," Brett said.

"You've got that right. Now maybe you'll be able to
concentrate on your homework for that psych course of
yours."

Brett was taking one class at Loyola that met Monday
and Wednesday afternoons. She left Hope with Frieda and
Consuela for baby-sitting while she was at school. Even
though Hope was now wary of strangers, she recognized
the older women next door as adopted grandmothers, and
they acted the part to the hilt.

While Brett was reflecting, Hope was reaching again. A
second later, the little girl had put wet handprints all over
the paper Brett was working on for class. Looking and
grabbing had been perfected to a fine art by the eight-

month-old, who did it with split-second timing, only to have everything end up in her mouth.

"Think my professor will buy the excuse that the baby ate my homework?" Brett wryly asked as she held up the soggy sheet of paper.

"I doubt it."

Frustrated that Brett had taken her paper "plaything" away, Hope yelled "Maaa-maaa!" along with a variety of baby sounds, all of them intended to show her displeasure.

"Do you think babies know how to swear?" Michael inquired dryly.

Instead of replying she said, "Did you see that?" as the little girl latched onto Brett's leg and hauled herself upright in an attempt to get her soggy paper back. "She'll be walking before we know it! She already kind of pulls herself upright by hanging onto the rungs of her crib. I caught her doing it just last night. And now she just did it again. You clever girl, you!" Brett congratulated her with one of the wet, sloppy kisses that Hope adored.

"Hey, you feel like giving me one of those?" Michael inquired suggestively.

"Sure thing, big guy," Brett replied. Scooping Hope up in her arms, she carried the baby over to him. Moments later the little girl was placing sloppy, smacking kisses all along Michael's forceful jaw.

"That wasn't quite what I had in mind," Michael noted ruefully.

Returning to her homework, Brett said, "Oh, did I tell you that the energy-efficient thermostat I installed on the boiler reduced the heating bill by twenty percent last month?"

"Yeah, you did. Selling this place is still my long-term plan, but it may take longer to fix it up than I first thought. A couple of years instead of just one. But it would be nice to have a big yard someday for Hope to play in when she starts doing football practice.''

''In your dreams. The football practice, I mean, not the yard.''

The strangled sound of the buzzer prevented him from answering.

''Finally,'' Brett said as she hurriedly buzzed them in.

''You didn't check to see who it was first,'' Michael reprimanded her as he played horsie with Hope on his knee. ''You fixed the busted speaker in that security system and then you forget to use it.''

''Because I know who it is. It's the delivery man with the pizza we ordered an hour ago. Five minutes longer and I would have fainted from hunger,'' she said as she opened the front door to find a young woman standing there.

''Are you Brett Munro?'' the woman asked.

Brett nodded before remembering she was Brett Janos now. ''And you are?''

''Here to get my baby.''

# Ten

Brett had to swallow twice before she was able to speak. Even then, her voice came out thin and reedy. "What did you say?"

"My baby girl. I left her here."

"Who is it, Brett?" Michael called out from the living room behind her.

"I left my baby girl here, in the foyer when you were working there," the woman said in a hurry.

Brett shook her head, unable to accept that her worst nightmare was actually here, standing on the threshold of their apartment.

Worried by her silence, Michael quickly put Hope in the playpen before joining her at the door. "Who are you?" he demanded of the strange young woman in a black leather jacket.

"My name is Denise Petty."

"She says she's Hope's mother," Brett whispered.

"Hope?" The woman repeated. "I left my baby girl Angela here. It was wrong of me, I know. But I was desperate. I'd gotten into a bad situation.... I didn't want to put my baby at risk. My kid sister hangs out at the youth center, she's always raving about you. Maybe you remember her, bright kid with a bad dye job? Anyway from what she said, I figured you'd be the best place to leave my little girl until I could come back and get her."

Knowing her fears, Michael put a hand on Brett's shoulder and whispered, "Don't worry. She's not taking Hope from us."

His voice hardened as he spoke to the young woman. "You say your name is Denise? Well, Denise, what proof do you have that any of this is true?" Michael demanded.

"I brought Angela's birth certificate." She dug it out of the ratty woven bag she had slung over her shoulder.

Michael read the crumpled document carefully. "This doesn't prove that Angela is the same baby."

"She has a birthmark, a tiny red mark in the shape of a rose on her bottom," Denise said.

"Which side?" Michael demanded.

"Left side. I have one too, lower down." Lifting the hem of her already short black leather skirt, she showed them the mark on her thigh several inches above her knee.

Brett's heart dropped to her toes.

"What was the baby wearing when you left her here?" Michael asked.

"A sleeper outfit. And she had her blanket, the one with kittens on it. She was in a gray car safety seat for babies."

Looking at Brett, he saw her nod, confirming that was correct.

"I need that birth certificate back," Denise told Michael.

Reluctantly he handed it over. "What makes you think you can come waltzing in here and expect to get your baby back after abandoning her for months?"

"I don't expect anything," the young woman replied, sniffing back the tears that threatened to make her double coat of mascara run down her pale face. "I just want to make sure my little girl is fine."

"She's fine," Brett whispered huskily. "Would you like to come in a minute, have some tea or something?"

Michael looked at Brett as if she were out of her mind as she put an arm around the trembling young woman and guided her to the chair closest to the front door.

"I don't want anything, thanks," Denise said. "I don't mean to be a nuisance."

"I know." Brett patted her shoulder reassuringly. "Do you think you can tell us what happened, what made you do what you did?"

As Brett listened to Denise's story, which was an all too familiar one, full of bad decisions and rotten luck, something just didn't ring true.

Denise ended her sad tale by saying, "I ran out of money and couldn't take care of my little girl any more."

Whereupon Michael said, "So you want us to continue to take care of her. Adopt her, maybe?"

"Oh, no. She's mine. I couldn't give her up."

"And it doesn't look like you can take care of her, either."

"If I had more money I could." Jumping up and slipping past Michael, the woman rushed to the playpen, where she grabbed Hope. Picking her up, she hugged the little girl, who immediately started crying.

"Put the baby down," he ordered in a tone of voice that had made grown men cringe.

The young woman gave him an openly defiant look before doing as he'd directed.

Brett rushed over to soothe the upset baby while Michael took Denise aside. Handing her his business card, he said, "Come to my office tomorrow afternoon and bring that birth certificate with you, along with every other piece of identification you've got.''

"You can't keep my baby without my permission," Denise said, her previous timid demeanor replaced with a swagger he suspected was more in keeping with her normal personality.

"First off, I intend to verify that she really is your baby.''

"I already told you...."

"And I'm telling you that it won't hurt you to wait until tomorrow.''

"You better bring my baby to the meeting," Denise stated a low voice that was clearly a warning. "Otherwise I'll go to the authorities and tell them you've kidnapped her.''

"Child abandonment is a serious crime in this state," Michael retorted. "I don't think you want to involve the authorities.''

"I don't want to, but I will if you try and double-cross me. You can count on it, mister." Any trace of tears had long since disappeared, replaced by a sneer that twisted her brightly colored lips. She walked out, her three-inch heels clicking on the wood floor. Michael closed the door behind her, vowing to find out everything there was to know about Denise Petty before another twenty-four hours had gone by.

"Oh, Michael, what are we going to do?" Brett asked in a trembling voice as she held Hope in her arms, her hand cradling the little girl's head protectively.

"I can tell you what we're *not* going to do. We're not going to panic. And we're not handing Hope over to that woman.''

"We can't keep a baby from her real mother.''

"What makes you think that woman was any kind of good mother?''

"I don't know what to think," Brett whispered.

"I can't believe you invited her into our home. And I can't believe that you're even thinking of handing Hope over to that woman!"

"That woman is Hope's mother."

"You're out of your mind, do you know that? The way you were treating her, offering her tea, practically offering her Hope on a silver platter. What's the matter, are you tired of taking care of the baby already?"

She looked at him with stricken eyes. "How can you say that? I love Hope more than anything."

"So do I. And I plan on fighting to keep her!"

Putting a calmed-down Hope back in her playpen, Brett handed her a plastic key ring which was a favorite toy of hers, before speaking to Michael again. But by now anger replaced her pain as she glared at him. "How dare you insinuate that I'm tired of looking after Hope!" Infuriated, she socked his arm. "Where the hell did that come from?"

Rubbing his arm, he frowned. "I don't know," he muttered. "I know how much you love Hope."

"Have I ever done anything to indicate that I was tired of her?"

"No, you're great with her. I panicked, okay? The thought of that woman walking off with our baby made me panic for a minute. And you've got such a soft heart, you'd give someone the coat right off your back."

"Well, I don't plan on handing Hope over on a silver platter, okay? I'm not *that* generous. Not by a long shot. Do you have any idea how much that little girl means to me?" Her voice quavered.

"I know. I was an idiot. I'm sorry I hurt you," he murmured, running his fingers down her cheek. "I'd rather cut off my right arm than do that."

"Keep your right arm. We might need it to fight off the dragon lady."

Her irritated description made him laugh. "So you didn't like her, either?"

"There was just something about her... And then there was the way Hope cried when Denise picked her up. Granted, Hope is going through this period now where she has separation anxiety...."

Michael knew how that felt. He was secretly worried that he and Brett would be separated somehow.

"But still you'd think she'd have some memory of her mother," Brett continued. "Even if she didn't, I didn't like the way Denise held Hope. I didn't sense a lot of caring there."

"Good. Then you're with me about fighting her."

"I don't know how successful we can be. We always knew there was the possibility that Hope's real mother would come back for her."

"Yeah, we should have prepared for this eventuality. I guess both of us were enjoying the world we'd made too much to want to disturb the dream."

Did that mean he thought they'd only been playing house while the reality was that Hope wasn't really theirs? Had the happiness they'd shared these past weeks just been a fool's paradise? If so, Denise's arrival had brought them down to earth with a crash.

"I read on the birth certificate that Hope was born on June 1st," Michael said. "That means you judged her age right on the money."

His words brought tears to her eyes. "Oh, Michael. What are we going to do if she takes Hope away?"

"We won't let her."

But his words didn't console Brett. Even being in his arms couldn't comfort her, couldn't erase the terror striking her heart.

What would she do if she lost Hope? How could she survive such a loss? Brett's panic ran so deep, she couldn't even cry, much as she wanted to. It was terrifying to think how fragile her happiness had been, built on dreams.

She lacked the blind faith to believe everything would work out in the end—it never had in the past, not unless she'd worked and fought for it.

*Don't be a nuisance, Brett.*

*Why do you always have to want more?*

*I need a woman who can be a real wife.*

Her past was there again, nipping at her heels and eating away at her self-confidence.

Was this what she got for wanting too much? She'd had a family, but she'd wanted more. She'd wanted Michael to love her. A physical attraction hadn't been enough. And now look what had happened—she could lose everything.

Michael had just made some headway in his efforts to pull every bit of information on Denise Petty from his office computer when the phone rang. Denise hadn't shown up, and he hadn't brought little Hope to the office. Stalemate.

He had to be missing something....

His secretary buzzed him. "Collect call for you on line one."

"Who's it from?" he demanded, annoyed at the interruption.

"I couldn't make out the name."

Muttering under his breath, Michael punched the blinking extension button.

A tinny message said, "Collect call from..." There was a pause as the recorded message was inserted: "Juan."

"Will you accept the charges?" the operator asked.

"No. I don't know anyone named Juan."

Slamming down the phone, Michael's attention immediately went back to his computer screen. Two minutes later Lorraine buzzed him again. "What?"

"Collect call on line one. Claims it's an emergency."

Thinking it might be Brett, he grabbed the phone, impatiently waiting for the tinny message before the recorded section said "Juan-Brett's-friend-from-the-youth-center-about-Brett" all in one rush.

"Yes, I'll accept the call," Michael told the operator. "Has something happened to Brett?" he demanded of Juan. "Is she hurt?"

"Not yet, but she could be," Juan replied.

"What the hell is that supposed to mean? Is that some kind of threat?"

"Man, you are so ignorant! Brett is too good for you!" Juan retorted.

"Just tell me what's going on."

"Not over the phone. Come meet me at the youth center. In half an hour. It's about Brett...and that baby you're keeping, the one that was left on your doorstep."

The next sound Michael heard was the dial tone. Swearing under his breath, he grabbed his coat from the coat rack and headed out the door.

"Where are you going?" Lorraine demanded.

"Personal business."

"That's all you seem to be doing lately. At this rate you're not going to have any clients left."

"Considering the fact that I've worked my butt off for my clients every day since I took over this faltering business, I think they could cut me a little slack here. That goes for you, too."

"Ah, it's good to have your old fighting self back," Lorraine said approvingly. "You've been brooding up a storm all day. Not at all like your old self. Besides, you've got enough business as it is."

"Listen, while I'm gone, get that security report done up for Anderson Construction. The cassette is on my desk."

"With a voice like yours, you should be reading those books on tape, not dictating security recommendations," she told him for the umpteenth time.

"Yeah, right. If my wife calls, be sure and have me paged."

It was only three o'clock, but heavy traffic and sleet turned a twenty-five minute trip to St. Gerald's into a forty-minute one. Throughout it, Michael's thoughts remained on his newfound family and what part Juan played in all this. What if the kid was just being a smart-ass, leading him on some juvenile wild-goose chase?

Squeezing his car into the nearest parking space, Michael ran into the youth center, nearly sliding on the slippery pavement as he yanked open the door.

"You're late," Juan said from just inside.

"Listen, you're lucky I chased out here at all," Michael growled, his patience at an end. "This better be damn good!"

"It will be worth your while," was all Juan said. "There's someone I want you to meet."


Brett shifted her book bag as she climbed the steps to her building's front door. She'd almost skipped her Wednesday class, wanting to stay home with Hope and hold her tight so that no one could take her away. But Michael had convinced her that wouldn't be the best thing to do. After all, she'd only be gone three hours. So she'd left, only to worry about Hope the whole time. As she walked into the building, her fears were intensified by the crowd waiting for her in the hallway—Mr. and Mrs. Stephanopolis, Frieda and Consuela and Keisha. The only one missing was Tyrone. And Hope.

"What's wrong? Is it Hope? Did something happen to her?" Brett demanded, her heart in her throat, squeezing the words as she tried to get them out.

"Hope is fine," Frieda hurriedly reassured her. "Consuela is watching over her while she naps."

"Is it Michael? Did something happen to Michael?"

"Not as far we as know," Frieda replied.

"But something did happen," Mr. Stephanopolis said.

"Don't leave the girl in suspense," his wife declared. "Just tell her someone tried to kidnap her baby."

"So much for breaking it to her gently," Frieda muttered.

"What?" Brett gasped. "Someone tried to kidnap Hope?"

"They tried to snatch her right out of her bounce chair," Frieda said.

"How did they get into your apartment?"

"Well, she said she was a friend of yours when she knocked at my door. She was wearing a black leather jacket and enough mascara and eyeliner to sink a battleship."

That sounded like Denise, all right. "How did she even get into the building?"

"That's my fault, I'm afraid," Mrs. Stephanopolis inserted. "I had so many groceries to carry that I propped the outer door open with a flagstone. Apparently she slipped inside while I was upstairs."

"When I told her that you were at class, she practically pushed herself into our living room and snatched the baby from her bounce chair. She was all ready to run out the door but I blocked her. That's when Consuela came in, waving her cooking spoon and shouting for the woman to put Hope down or we'd call the police."

"Did you call the police?" Brett asked.

Frieda shook her head. "Keisha came in at that point."

Keisha promptly picked up the storytelling. "I heard all the commotion as I walked in the building. The door to their place was still open, so I went in and saw what was going on. I grabbed the perp...."

"Stop with the cop-show talk," Frieda protested.

"We restrained the suspect," Keisha said.

"They retrained her?" Mr. Stephanopolis said with a tap to his hearing aid. "I gotta get a new battery for this darn thing."

"You better sit down, you look pale," Frieda told Brett.

"I want to see Hope."

Nodding understandingly, Frieda ushered Brett into their apartment, opened the bedroom door and showed where Hope was sleeping. Consuela was watching over her, doing some needlework as she rocked in the rocking chair.

Brett didn't realize she'd been holding her breath until that moment. Only when she touched her baby's soft arm did she relax. Hope *was* hers—not by right of biology, but by right of love. And no one was going to steal her. No way! She'd fight to the death to protect what was hers.

Gathering her composure, Brett kissed the little girl's dimpled cheek before returning to the living room, whereupon Mr. Stephanopolis said, "Did you tell her about the part where I came down with my big fishing net and snagged her? Biggest fish I ever did catch," he declared with a laugh.

Brett closed her eyes. This was beginning to sound like a Keystone Kops episode.

"Where is she now?" she asked.

"Keisha has her cuffed to the radiator in your old apartment downstairs," Frieda admitted.

"I had to stick a sock in her mouth to shut her up," Keisha said.

"How long has she been there?"

"Only a few minutes. This just happened. We were getting ready to call the police when you came home."

"There's no need to call the police," Brett said. "I know the woman. I'm sorry she caused such a scene, and I dearly appreciate your going to such lengths to protect Hope."

"We said we'd take care of her while you were at class," Frieda stated. "Of course we'd protect her. We've heard stories on TV about babies being snatched and never found again. We weren't about to let that happen to little Hope."

"I'd better go down and talk to the woman," Brett said. "Who is she?"

Brett didn't know how to answer that. If she told them the truth, they might call the police. Handcuffing and gagging Hope's real mother in the basement wouldn't look good to the authorities.

"She's someone I know," Brett finally replied.

"She has mental problems if you ask me," Frieda declared. "Her eyes were set close together. Never a good sign."

"Come on, I'll go downstairs with you," Keisha said, putting an arm around Brett. Once they were on the relative privacy of the stairs, Keisha softly confessed, "I figured you wouldn't want the police involved. I heard the woman when she was here yesterday. I was coming up from the basement with the wash when she stood outside your door and said she was Hope's mother. It may not have been smart to cuff her to the radiator, but I didn't know what else to do. I didn't want her taking off with that baby. She looked like trouble. Not the maternal type, you know what I mean?"

Brett nodded. "I really appreciate this, Keisha," she whispered unsteadily.

"Don't go gettin' sentimental on me now, girl. We got to face this wild woman in the basement first."

Brett's old apartment looked cold and empty, but the hatred emanating from Denise Petty's eyes was laser-hot. When Brett removed the sock from her mouth, Denise spewed a string of venomous curses before Keisha held up the sock threateningly. "You shut your mouth, girl, or I'll shut it for you."

"You're going to be sorry you ever messed with me," Denise spat, reaching out to try and slap Keisha, who wisely stood out of reach since the other woman was still cuffed to the radiator.

Acting as peacemaker, Brett said, "Calm down, Denise. I know you're upset right now, but I'm sure we can work things out."

"What planet are you living on?" Denise retorted.

But Brett knew exactly what she was doing. She'd worked with troublemakers like Denise before. "I know you didn't really mean to scare everyone."

Sensing that Brett was now on her side, Denise sent Keisha a triumphant look before lowering her eyes, and her voice. "That's right. I just came to see my daughter."

"Where were you going to take her?"

"To a friend's house. I wasn't going to hurt her. I was going to bring her back if..."

"If?" Brett prompted. "Go on, Denise. I know you're smart. You must have had a plan."

"If I couldn't take care of her myself."

"You're good," Brett acknowledged. "I'd almost believe you if it weren't for your eyes. I know the kids at the youth center think I'm a naive optimist, but trust me, Denise, I'm not. I know you're lying, so why don't you save us both some trouble and tell me the truth."

"I'm telling you the truth. She's my kid. It's not like I was kidnapping her or anything. She's mine and if I want to get some money out of the deal, that's my business!"

"You tried to steal her for the money?"

"She's my kid. I was going to bring her back...for the right price."

Brett's expression hardened. "How much?"

"Twenty thousand."

"Yeah, you seem like the kind of scum that would sell their own baby," Keisha said in disgust. "And you call yourself a mother?"

"That's what she calls herself," Michael drawled from the doorway. "But it isn't the truth. She is *not* Hope's mother."

# Eleven

Brett stared at her husband in amazement. "What did you say?"

"You heard me," Michael replied as he entered the room with Juan at his side. "She's *not* Hope's mother."

"But she has the same birthmark, and she knew all the details about the day Hope was left in our foyer," Brett said.

"That's because she was with Hope's mother when she left the baby here."

"And the birthmark?" Brett demanded.

"Is shared by all the girls in the Petty family," Michael replied. "It turns out that Denise here is really Darlene, Denise's twin sister. They weren't identical twins, but they looked enough alike for Darlene to take over her sister's identity when she was killed in a hit-and-run accident a few weeks ago."

"Hope's real mother was killed?" Brett whispered.

"That's right. Tell her what you told me, Juan."

Juan said, "See, I'm friends like with their younger sister, Linda. She's scared of Darlene, but she confided in me. She said she couldn't stand to see you hurt, Brett. She said you were too good for that. So she told me, even though Darlene threatened to beat her if she told anyone."

"That little traitor!" Darlene screeched. "Wait 'til I get my hands on her, I'll teach her to snitch on me!"

Juan ignored the outburst. "Hope's real mother was Denise, the good sister."

"Yeah, the angel in the family," Darlene said, her face twisted with hatred. "Always the perfect one, the one who could do no wrong. Until she got herself knocked up. And even then, my mom didn't kick her out of the house like she did me."

"Because you went after her with a frying pan," Juan said. "Linda told me all about it."

"I'll knock that girl's teeth out," Darlene snarled.

"Put a sock in it, Darlene," Brett advised.

Taking her literally, Keisha did just that, effectively halting the string of curses Darlene was spouting by stuffing the sock back in the woman's mouth.

Only then did someone else slip into the room, a young girl Brett recognized from the youth center. "Linda?"

The girl nodded.

Brett held out her arms, and the frightened girl ran into them. "It'll be okay, honey. We'll make sure Darlene won't ever hurt you again," she murmured in a soothing voice.

"You've got that right," Michael said. "I did some checking of my own after Juan filled me in on the details. It turns out that while Denise Petty had a clean record, Darlene has had plenty of experience with breaking the law."

"Why didn't you find this out when you checked out her story on your computer this morning?" Brett asked.

"She didn't show for the meeting in my office, so I knew something was up. The problem was that Denise Petty was actually born *Donna* Denise Petty and her records were listed that way. I'd just discovered that when Juan here called me and had me come over to the youth center. That's when he told me about Darlene posing as her sister."

"Thanks for telling us, Juan," Brett said with a grateful smile.

"He also told me that she was planning on snatching Hope and holding her for ransom. So I rushed over here to save the day, but I see you already have things under control," Michael said. "Nice move, cuffing her to the radiator, by the way."

"It was Keisha's idea," Brett replied. "She captured Darlene."

"With help from the other tenants," Keisha said.

"Fast thinking, Keisha," Michael congratulated her. "When this is all over maybe you and I should have a little talk about you coming to work for me. I could use some help in the business."

Keisha beamed.

"Meanwhile, what do we do about Darlene?" Brett asked. "We can't just leave her here."

"Read this," Linda said, taking a school composition notebook from under her denim jacket and handing it to Brett. "Maybe it will help you make up your mind."

"What is it?"

"It's Denise's diary. She watched you, even though she never talked to you. And I told her about you. My mom drinks, and Denise didn't want her to ruin her baby's life like she . . ." Linda's voice trailed off in embarrassment. "Anyway, read what she wrote."

Brett did.

I took little Angela over there today and left her for Brett to find. Even though I've never met her, I can tell that she has a good heart. She'll do what's best for my baby. If she can't take care of Angela herself, she'll find a good family that can. Maybe I should have been brave and taken the baby to someplace official, an orphanage maybe, but I don't know where any are and I had to do something fast. Momma hit the baby today and I knew things would just get worse here. I don't want that for my Angela. This mess isn't her fault. Brett will know what to do, because I sure don't.

Brett swallowed back her tears. "What about the baby's father?" she asked unsteadily.

"Denise never said who he was," Linda replied. "Just that he didn't want any part of the baby and that he was involved in some pretty rough stuff. She said he'd moved to L.A."

Before Brett could say anything further, a knock on the partially open door to the apartment got everyone's attention. So did the pair of police officers who walked in. "We got a call about a disturbance here. Which one of you is Michael Janos?"

"I am," Michael said, stepping forward. "Thanks for getting here so fast, officers."

"You called the police?" Brett whispered in alarm.

Putting a reassuring arm around her, Michael nodded. "As soon as Frieda told me that Denise...I mean Darlene here had tried to snatch Hope and was down here with you."

The officer looked at the gagged and handcuffed Darlene with disapproval. "Someone want to tell me what's going on here?"

"It's a long story," Michael said. "The bottom line is that the young woman being restrained is Darlene Petty and there's an outstanding warrant for her arrest in your files." To Brett he added, "You see, Darlene wanted the money to skip town because she's wanted by the police in a series of burglaries." Speaking to the officers again, Michael explained, "She's been pretending to be her twin sister Denise, and has her ID, but if you fingerprint her you'll find she is indeed Darlene."

After that, things seemed to happen very quickly in Brett's dazed opinion. Once the officers had confirmed that a warrant was outstanding, they removed Darlene with speed, adding resisting arrest to her charges as she kicked one of the officers with her pointed high heels before being bundled outside.

Once the police had taken Darlene away, Brett confessed one of her worries to Michael. "As Hope's aunt, she still may have a legal right to the baby."

"She never wanted her, she just wanted the money," he replied.

"She's going to tell them about Hope, I know she is."

"You've got that diary to prove that the baby's mother wanted you to take care of her. The judge is going to give her to us, Brett. We don't have to do anything but tell the truth."

As she went into his arms, Brett knew that the only truth she still couldn't tell was the fact that she loved him.

"'And they lived happily ever after,'" Brett read from the story she was telling Hope at bedtime that night.

She sat in the rocking chair with the little girl on her lap. The feel of the baby's head resting against her breast brought tears of relief to Brett's eyes. "I love you, Hope. I love you so much."

But Hope, who had another tooth coming in and didn't want to be fussed over too much, pushed her away.

*Don't be a nuisance, Brett.*

Feeling vulnerable because of the emotional roller coaster she'd been on today, Brett bit her lip as a sob silently shuddered through her.

As if sensing her mother's pain, the baby abruptly turned her head back toward Brett, and snuggled against her, giving her a semitoothless grin of such sweetness that Brett's sob was transformed into a tiny, poignant laugh.

"I never knew my own mother," Brett unsteadily confided to the little girl. "I never had anyone really mother me, so I'm not sure how good a job I'll do as a mom. But I promise to always love you, no matter what. And to try and give you guidance in this crazy world. Just don't expect too much from me, okay? I mean, I'll do the best I can, but I don't know if love is always enough, you know?"

The baby nodded, as if she understood every word.

"I mean, I love Michael and that doesn't mean..." Pausing, Brett fingered the golden hammer he'd given her for Christmas. She wore it on a chain under her sweater, against her bare skin. "It doesn't mean he loves me back. When you were almost taken away from us, I felt so guilty. Like God was punishing me for wanting too much, you know? So I made a deal with God—that if we got to keep you, I wouldn't ever ask for anything, ever again. And I'm going to keep that promise. But I don't want you ever doubting that Michael loves *you*, little one. Even when he's calling you stinky britches, he loves you. You're a lucky little girl to have such a great daddy. Not many kids have dads who play This Little Pig Went to The Play-offs on their toes. He made that up just for you. It's one of the ways he shows you how much he loves you. Like when he doesn't complain when you drool all over him. Or the way he gets so excited when you do something new. He's going to be the best daddy in the world to you, Hope. I just wish I could give him a baby of his own. He deserves that.

Since that's something I wish for Michael, I guess it doesn't break my promise to God, huh?''

Looking down, Brett realized that Hope had nodded off to sleep.

After safely tucking her in her crib for the night, Brett walked into the bedroom she shared with Michael to find him sitting on the edge of the bed. He turned to stare at her, his hazel eyes darkened by the turbulent intensity of his gaze.

"We need to talk," he said huskily.

She immediately knew something was wrong from the sound of his voice, but it wasn't until his gaze slid from her to the baby monitor on the bedside table that it clicked in her mind. The baby monitor. The thing was a damn microphone! She'd forgotten all about it when she'd spilled her heart out in the nursery. She'd forgotten it was there, picking up every word she'd said. He'd heard her.

Brett had never been so embarrassed in her entire life. She wished the floor would open up and suck her in.

*Don't be a nuisance, Brett.*

*Why do you always have to want more?*

*I need a woman who can be a real wife.*

The mocking, hurtful words from her past were right there to taunt her. But this time, something new happened. This time she fought, shoving the words from her the way Hope had shoved moments before.

Brett's courage bounced back, and with it came the realization that she was tired of apologizing for her past, for her emotions, for having hope.

Well, no more. No more hanging onto the past. She'd had to fight for everything she had—she was ready to fight now!

"That's right, I love you," she practically shouted. "You want to make something out of it?" she demanded, putting her hands on her hips to stare at him defiantly.

Michael was startled by her aggressive reaction. She saw that in those awesome eyes of his. And then she saw something else. Admiration?

"Damn right I want to make something out of it," he growled, holding out his hand to her. "Come here."

She took one step toward him before stopping. "No," she declared. "You can come here."

"Okay," he said.

Getting up, he was at her side in four steps, only to scoop her in his arms and dump her in the middle of the bed.

"How could you be so stupid?" he demanded, kneeling on the mattress beside her.

"I fought it, believe me," she declared in irritation. "Blame it on that damn Rom box of yours. That or your incredible eyes . . ."

He put his finger to her lips, silencing her. "How could you think I don't love you?"

She stared at him as if he'd grown two heads. Pulling his hand away, she said, "Excuse me?"

"I said, how could you think for one minute that I don't love you?"

"I don't know," she shot back. "Maybe the fact that you never told me you loved me had something to do with it."

He grimaced at her direct verbal hit. "Okay, so I didn't say the words, but I showed you. I sent you acorns, even seduced you on my office desk, for God's sake. How many women do you think I've done that to?"

"I have no idea. And I'm not sure I want to know. . . ."

"None, that's how many," he growled. "I love you."

She blinked at him uncertainly. "Do you have that Rom box in the bedroom again?"

"Forget the damn box. I am not under a spell."

"Right. Like you'd know if you were."

"What is it going to take to convince you?" he demanded in exasperation.

"I don't know. Maybe fifty years of your life."

"Deal," he whispered, sealing his pledge with a teasing kiss, the merest brushing of her lips with his. "Why is it so hard for you to believe that I love you?" he murmured.

"Maybe because no one else has loved me before," she whispered.

"Brett, there are plenty of people who love you. You've touched so many people's lives."

"That's nothing."

"It is not nothing. I know your mother left you, and that bastard of a fiancé left you. But look at me...." With gentle fingers he grasped her chin and turned her face so that he could look directly into her eyes. "I'm not like them. I'm not going to leave you. If you want to believe that a Rom love spell charmed us both, then believe it. And know that magic is a powerful thing, not to be trifled with. It will bind us together no matter what. It will last a lifetime."

"Are you kidding?"

"Do I look like I'm kidding?" he returned.

He met her gaze head-on. She saw...she saw love there. Love for her!

"I didn't know you loved me," he whispered. "Not until tonight when I heard you confessing to Hope."

"How could you not know?" she said in disbelief. "I practically drooled whenever you came in the room. I seduced you on New Year's Eve."

"That didn't mean you loved me."

"I married you."

"For the baby's sake. I knew you loved her. I knew you'd do anything for her, including marrying me if that meant you'd get to keep Hope."

"I thought that's why you married me. To save Hope."

"I married you because I had to have you."

She nodded understandingly. "The love charm . . ."

"*You* charmed me. It was *you*. The way you light up a room with your smile, the way you embrace life, the way you care about others, the way you look in those damn tight jeans, the way your big blue eyes glow when you talk, the way your laugh sounds like an angel's song." He broke off self-consciously.

"Don't stop now, you were doing fine," Brett said with a smile bright enough to illuminate downtown Chicago.

"Do you believe me?"

"I want to."

"What's stopping you?"

"Why didn't you tell me you loved me before?"

"First off, like I said, I didn't know if you loved me."

"So you were waiting for me to say it first?" She smacked his shoulder with the palm of her hand. "How like a man!"

"I told you when I proposed that I wasn't good with emotions," he muttered. "I may come from an emotional family, but I've never found it easy to talk about my emotions, okay? It was hard for me to come out and say it."

"Like it was easy for me?"

"You didn't say it to me," he retorted. "You didn't tell me you loved me, you told stinky britches and it's pretty damn certain the secret would be safe with her."

"How can I be sure you love me for real?"

"I guess you can't be sure. You have to follow your heart, and give yourself fifty years or so to be convinced."

Time stood still as their eyes met. No other man had ever looked at her in quite that way, as if she'd unlocked the deepest secrets of his heart and held the key to his happiness.

With an unsteady cry of happiness, Brett threw her arms around him, tumbling them both back onto the mattress.

She eagerly sought his mouth, meeting him halfway as he lifted his head to kiss her. His need matched her own.

But there was more than just need in this kiss. More than desire or passion. There was the freedom of two hearts joined as one. There was no holding back on either of their parts. Brett felt gloriously free to show her love, to whisper it as she unbuttoned his shirt and ran her hands down his chest. When he whispered his love for her, her joy knew no bounds. He told her over and over again, showed her with every brush of his mouth, every tender caress of his hands.

Clothing—hers and his—flew in every direction. The rough moistness of his tongue circling her nipple diverted her from her explorations of the lean hardness of his body. Excitement shot through her, heightening her craving to have him lodged within her. "Now," she whispered, as she reached for him. "Don't make me wait...."

With one electrifying thrust he made her his, joining them in a union that was both physical and spiritual. Leashing his own ardor, he made sure to satisfy her first. She could feel the muscles of his thighs flexing against her own as he rocked against her.

The anticipation was strong, building deep within her, deeper than ever before, stirring and soaring, expanding and contracting, rippling waves that grew... and grew... intensifying with every sliding thrust of his body.

Her breath caught, and she dug her fingers into his shoulders at the sensations flaring within her. Brett had the feeling of being suspended, poised on the knife-edge of a pleasure so sharply intense it was almost a pain, a delicious addictive pain that instantly overflowed into joyful pulsing surges so powerful she cried out in a primal display of ultimate feminine fulfillment.

Gasping her name, Michael threw his head back as he froze above her, prolonging the moment as long as he could before his climax overcame him and sent him tumbling into her welcoming arms.

"I have a small cabin in the mountains in North Carolina. If you want, we could go there for a belated honeymoon," Michael said much later. They lay together, their legs entwined, her cheek resting on his chest, just above his heartbeat. "It's nothing fancy...."

"I don't need anything fancy," she assured him, kissing the line of his jaw. "But if you don't mind, I'd rather stay here. I've got everything I want right here."

Tilting her face up to his, he kissed her before murmuring, "If I had to do it all over again there's only one thing I'd do differently... well, two things."

"What are they?"

"I'd tell you I love you sooner... and I'd marry you in a big family wedding."

*One month later...*

"I now pronounce you husband and wife," Father Lyden said. "You may kiss..."

Michael had lifted Brett's veil and lowered his lips to hers before the priest had even finished speaking. His lips covered hers with seductive devotion and devilish adoration. Brett no longer doubted that he loved her. She knew it, just as she knew how much she loved him more every day.

She didn't hear the sound of Father Lyden clearing his throat, she didn't hear the laughter of those in the church. But she did hear her daughter, Hope Angela Janos, squealing at the top of her lungs.

"The ink isn't even dry on her adoption papers and already she's making trouble," Michael muttered as he broke off the kiss.

"She wants her daddy," Brett noted. "I want him, too," she added with a saucy grin before turning to face the congregation.

Brett wore the same dress she'd worn at city hall, only this time they'd exchanged their vows in front of a congregation filled with friends and family. Juan and Linda were there, as was Michael's secretary Lorraine. Also present and teary-eyed were all the tenants from Love Street—Mr. and Mrs. Stephanopolis, Frieda and Consuela. Keisha stood up as her matron of honor, while Michael's brother, dark-eyed Dylan, was the groom's best man, having flown in all the way from Arizona, his third state in as many months. The entire Janos family had shown up, with plenty of distant cousins and friends of the family.

Instead of presents, the new couple asked that donations be made to St. Gerald's Youth Center. At the reception given at Michael's parents' house, Father Lyden said he'd received enough money to begin renovations on the old gym.

There was much celebrating, topped by toasts of *pálinka*. By now, Brett was proud to be able to say the traditional toast of *Egészégére* like a native, much to the delight of her in-laws. She could even down the shot glass of chilled pear brandy without choking on it.

Brett liked Michael's younger brother, who seemed to be full of the devil, but she worried about Gaylynn, who had just recently taken a leave of absence from her teaching job in the inner city, saying she had burnt out. Her haunted eyes attested to that fact. Gaylynn was leaving right after the reception, driving down to stay in Michael's cabin in North Carolina. Brett hoped the change of scenery would do her good.

"If you two don't mind, I'm going to head on out now," Gaylynn was telling them. "It's getting late and I've got a long drive."

"You could always wait until tomorrow...." Michael began, in his big-brother voice.

Brett put her hand on his arm. "Don't you have something you want to give your sister before she leaves?"

"Yeah." Michael gave Gaylynn one of his trademark bear hugs. "Have a good trip, kiddo. Oh, yeah, and take this with you." He handed her a closed cardboard box.

"What is it?" Gaylynn asked.

Knowing what was inside, Brett smiled as Michael said, "Just a little something from the Old Country to bring you luck."

After she'd left, Brett said, "Do you think she'll be all right?"

"I'll have my friend Hunter check in on her."

"Should we have warned her about the Rom box?"

Michael shook his head. "She already knows the legend."

"That's more than I did."

"You don't still think I married you because of that love charm, do you?"

"I think I'm very glad that I was the first woman you looked at."

"You're the only woman I'll look at," he said, bending to kiss her. "You sure you're not sorry about skipping a honeymoon for now?"

Turning slightly in his arms, she watched as her mother-in-law held Hope by the hand as the baby took faltering steps toward Consuela. The little girl couldn't walk by herself yet, but the time was soon coming. And Brett didn't want to miss a minute of it. "No, I'm not sorry," she said huskily. "I'm not sorry about anything, not when I've finally gotten everything I ever hoped for."

"Have I told you today how much I love you?" Michael whispered in her ear.

*Now* Brett felt married. "I just hope the box brings your sister as much love as it did us," she whispered as she stepped into her husband's welcoming embrace.

\*   \*   \*   \*   \*

# For the Janos siblings

*Three Weddings and a Gift*

leads to a lot of loving!
Join award-winning author

# Cathie Linz

as she shows how an *unusual* inheritance leads to
love at first sight—and beyond!—in

**MICHAEL'S BABY** #1023
September 1996

**SEDUCING HUNTER** #1029
October 1996

and

**ABBIE AND THE COWBOY** #1036
November 1996

Only from

SILHOUETTE® *Desire®*

## MILLION DOLLAR SWEEPSTAKES
## AND EXTRA BONUS PRIZE DRAWING

**SILHOUETTE®**

*Desire®*

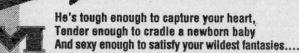

He's tough enough to capture your heart,
Tender enough to cradle a newborn baby
And sexy enough to satisfy your wildest fantasies....

He's Silhouette Desire's MAN OF THE MONTH!

From the moment he meets the woman of his
dreams to the time the handsome hunk says *I do*...

Fall in love with these incredible men:

In July:  *THE COWBOY AND THE KID*
by **Anne McAllister**

In August:  *DON'T FENCE ME IN*
by **Kathleen Korbel**

In September:  *TALLCHIEF'S BRIDE*
by **Cait London**

In October:  *THE TEXAS BLUE NORTHER*
by **Lass Small**

In November:  *STRYKER'S WIFE*
by **Dixie Browning**

In December:  *CHRISTMAS PAST*
by **Joan Hohl**

**MAN OF THE MONTH...ONLY FROM
SILHOUETTE DESIRE**

### SILHOUETTE®

# Desire®

September's MAN OF THE MONTH title

## TALLCHIEF'S BRIDE
Book 2 of

by bestselling author
## CAIT LONDON

All Calum Tallchief wanted was a nice, traditional
wife and a couple of kids to fill his lonely home in
Amen Flats, Wyoming. But the least likely woman
to be his wife was somehow wearing the Tallchief
ring, sharing his bedroom, gossiping with his relatives
and dreaming of motherhood...all without any
intention of becoming his bride!

What is September's MAN OF THE MONTH to do?

Don't miss the sexy second book of **The Tallchiefs**
miniseries by Cait London, available in September,
only from Silhouette Desire.

# As seen on TV!
## *Free Gift Offer*

With a Free Gift proof-of-purchase from any Silhouette® book,
you can receive a beautiful cubic zirconia pendant.

This gorgeous marquise-shaped stone is a genuine cubic
zirconia—accented by an 18" gold tone necklace.

(Approximate retail value $19.95)

## Send for yours today...
### compliments of ▼ *Silhouette*®
™

To receive your free gift, a cubic zirconia pendant, send us one original proof-of-
purchase, photocopies not accepted, from the back of any Silhouette Romance™,
Silhouette Desire®, Silhouette Special Edition®, Silhouette Intimate Moments®
or Silhouette Yours Truly™ title available in August, September or October at your favorite
retail outlet, together with the Free Gift Certificate, plus a check or money order for
$1.65 U.S./$2.15 CAN. (do not send cash) to cover postage and handling, payable
to Silhouette Free Gift Offer. We will send you the specified gift. Allow 6 to 8 weeks for
delivery. Offer good until October 31, 1996 or while quantities last. Offer valid in the
U.S. and Canada only.

## *Free Gift Certificate*

Name: _____

Address: _____

City: _____ State/Province: _____ Zip/Postal Code: _____

Mail this certificate, one proof-of-purchase and a check or money order for postage
and handling to: SILHOUETTE FREE GIFT OFFER 1996. In the U.S.: 3010 Walden
Avenue, P.O. Box 9077, Buffalo NY 14269-9077. In Canada: P.O. Box 613, Fort Erie,
Ontario L2Z 5X3.

---

### FREE GIFT OFFER
084-KMD

ONE PROOF-OF-PURCHASE

To collect your fabulous FREE GIFT, a cubic zirconia pendant, you must include this
original proof-of-purchase for each gift with the properly completed Free Gift Certificate.

---

084-KMD

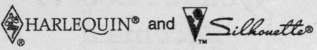

**HARLEQUIN® and Silhouette®**

are proud to present...

## HERE COME THE GROOMS™

Four marriage-minded stories written by top Harlequin and Silhouette authors!

Next month, you'll find:

| | |
|---|---|
| *Married?!* | by Annette Broadrick |
| *Designs on Love* | by Gina Wilkins |
| *It Happened One Night* | by Marie Ferrarella |
| *Lazarus Rising* | by Anne Stuart |

**ADDED BONUS!** In every edition of *Here Come the Grooms* you'll find $5.00 worth of coupons good for Harlequin and Silhouette products.

On sale at your favorite Harlequin and Silhouette retail outlet.

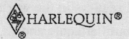

# You're About to Become a *Privileged Woman*

Reap the rewards of fabulous free gifts and benefits with proofs-of-purchase from Silhouette and Harlequin books

# Pages & Privileges™

It's our way of thanking you for buying our books at your favorite retail stores.

PROOF OF PURCHASE
SD-PP172
Offer expires October 31, 1996

Harlequin and Silhouette—
the most privileged readers in the world!

For more information about Harlequin and Silhouette's PAGES & PRIVILEGES program call the Pages & Privileges Benefits Desk: 1-503-794-2499

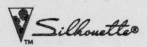

SD-PP172